POLIHALE
and other Kaua'i legends

POLIHALE
and other Kaua'i legends

FREDERICK B. WICHMAN

ILLUSTRATIONS BY CHRISTINE FAYÉ

BAMBOO RIDGE PRESS
1991

Library of Congress Catalog Card Number 91-24204
ISBN 0-910043-24-8

Four of these stories, Hina-Hau-Kaekae, Nā Mai'a O Manuahi,
Ka Pā'ū Onaona O Hina and Naupaka appeared in *Kauai Magazine*
and are reprinted here with their permission.

Published by Bamboo Ridge Press

Designed by Steve Shrader

Printed in the United States

This project has been supported in part by the State Foundation
on Culture and the Arts, the Robert E. Black Memorial Trust
of the Hawaii Community Foundation, and the McInerny Foundation.

This is a special double issue of *Bamboo Ridge, The Hawaii Writers' Quarterly*,
No. 53-54, ISSN 0733-0308.

Bamboo Ridge Press
P.O. Box 61781
Honolulu, Hawaii 96839-1781

8   7   6   5   4   02   03   04   05   06

Wichman, Frederick B.
    Polihale and other Kaua'i legends / written by Frederick B.
Wichman; illustrated by Christine Fayé.
        p. cm.
    "A special double issue (#53-54) of Bamboo ridge, the Hawaii
writers' quarterly"—T.p. verso.
    ISBN 0-910043-24-8 : $10.00
    1. Legends—Hawaii—Kauai.   2. Hawaiians—Folklore.   I. Bamboo
ridge.   Special issue.   II. Title.
GR110.H38W5   1991   91-24204
398.2'09969'4—dc20   CIP

CONTENTS

Dedicated to
my grandchildren

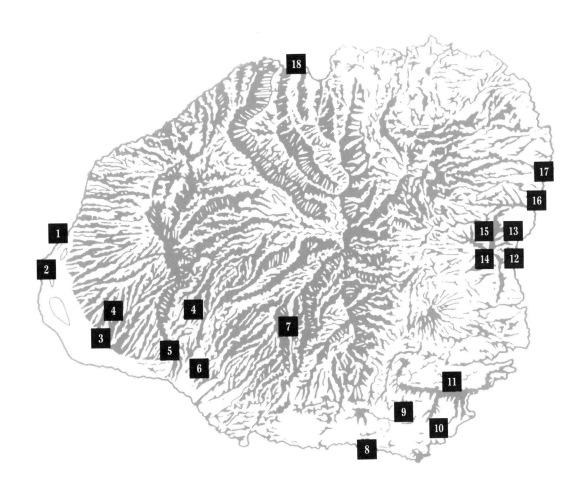

POLIHALE

CHRISTINE FAYÉ 91

er face was as bright as the full moon, her eyes sparkled like the stars of heaven and the chanters of songs compared Nā-pihe-nui to the beauty of the forest lehua tree in full bloom that attracts the 'apapane, the honeycreepers that flock to feed on the sweet nectar exuded by the flowers. Already there were young men coming to ask her father to give her in marriage.

Polihale took these proposals seriously. He was the konohiki chief of Mānā, a land that stretched from the western cliffs of Nā Pali to the eastern boundary shared with Wai'awa. Mānā is a land of long white beaches with the ocean on one side and a large swamp that teemed with birds on the other. Inland of the marsh was a fertile strip of land where sweet potatoes and gourds were grown. Above these fields cliffs rose stiff backed, broken by wide valleys down which constantly flowed fresh spring or rain fed water. The ridges, covered with sandalwood and koa trees, stretched into the mountains wreathed with cold and misty rain.

Mānā itself was hot and the village lay in the steep sided valley of Hā'ele'ele where shadows from the steep cliffs cooled the houses in the late afternoon. The houses were built on platforms against the cliffs, and irrigation ditches led the stream in and out of taro fields. The people had learned to plant taro in rafts that floated on the waters of the marsh. Fish was taken from the sea, and the sea and sun combined to give salt. The koloa, the native duck, was caught in the marshes and u'wau the size of chickens were taken from their nests in the cliffs. Reeds and grasses needed for weaving mats and thatching houses grew in profusion. Polihale's people were content for there was enough to eat and their chief made no strange demands upon their time and labor. Polihale and his priests made all the correct prayers to the gods and Mānā prospered.

Attracted by the beauties of Nā-pihe-nui and of Mānā, young chiefs flocked to ask Polihale for his daughter in marriage. Polihale always asked his daughter what she thought of the lastest suitor but Nā-pihe-nui only laughed and paid no attention to the young men.

Instead she joined her women companions to swim each afternoon after their work was over. Sometimes they bathed in the pool at Hā'ele'ele. Sometimes they swam in the ocean pool at Puʻu-o-honu.

Three rainbows followed her everywhere she went and hovered above the trees when she rested in their shade or hovered in the air above the pools. Some said the rainbows circled about her house while she slept.

Near the black cliff of Nā Pali there was a small grove of trees and a beach of black sand that ringed a deep pool of fresh water. This secret spot was protected on two sides by steep ledges of rock over which a stream that rose from the shadows of the trees poured its cooling waters before rippling down the little ravine to the sea. Here Nā-pihe-nui and her friends were safe from all eyes and could laugh, swim, weave wreaths of ferns and reed mats, and tell stories while the late afternoon hours passed by happily.

As weeks and months passed, Nā-pihe-nui, intent on her work and on her friends, did not notice that Polihale became a very worried man.

Recently, Polihale had noticed a strange and disturbing sight on the mountain above Hāʻeleʻele. A large white and brown cloud sat at odd times of day or night on the ridges. Often it seemed to have no particular shape, yet sometimes it seemed like a dog, its eyes staring intently down at some spot near the sea at Mānā.

Sometimes Polihale fancied the eyes were looking at him and that worried him most of all. He did not like unexplained clouds in his land.

One evening, he asked Hōkū-helelei, "What is that cloud?"

Hōkū-helelei was his kahuna kilokilo, the priest who studied the omens of the sky. "Cloud?" asked Hōkū-helelei doubtfully, looking up at it. "Well, we shall see."

That night he studied the clouds and the way they moved over the ridges, turning to mist when they neared the brown and white cloud. He studied the pattern made by the wandering stars and listened to the wind of dawn as she swept across the channel from Niihau. He saw birds veer away from the mysterious cloud and the land shells whose singing usually whispered through the night were silent. He watched this cloud grow smaller and smaller within minutes and disappear, yet the birds still did not come back and the land shells did not begin singing again. Then he opened his calabash that was half-filled with the sacred water that had been brought on the first canoe of settlers several generations before and stared down into its depths for a long time. On the surface of the black stone at the bottom of the calabash he saw mirrored a cloud black on one side, white on the other. He saw a large black dog change into a small white dog and change back into the cloud. He realized that he was seeing a kupua, a supernatural being that could shift from one form to another. He prayed to the supreme god Kū but he saw only the clouds and the dogs pictured in his calabash.

At dawn he spoke to Polihale. "Kū sent me messages that I do not understand," he admitted, "and since the other gods, Kāne, Kanaloa, or Lono, have not come to Hawaii, they do not hear my prayers. A word of warning, however. Be careful of dogs. They may not be what they seem. I shall continue to search the skies and the omens." With that Polihale had to be content.

What Hōkū-helelei had seen in his calabash was indeed a cloud, a black dog, and a white dog. These were earthly forms of the god Kū, the only god that had come from Tahiti with the first voyagers. He was appealed to for help with rain and growth of crops and for help in fishing. He was also the god of medicine and sorcery. But most of all he liked war and warfare. He could take any form he wished but his favorites were this cloud and the two dog forms, and whenever he took these forms, he was known as Kū-'īlio-loa. In his cloud form, he roamed over the mountains and at night stretched himself from one peak to another or from the mountain height above to his home in a cave below.

He had seen the three rainbows moving from place to place in Mānā and that made him very curious. A rainbow marked only persons of extremely high rank. Kū-'īlio-loa decided to see for himself. When he saw that the rainbows arched over the head of a lovely woman, he decided to take her as his wife.

The following day, Nā-pihe-nui and her friends came to swim in their favorite pool. The afternoon hours passed in cheerful conversation and laughter and diving into the pool to escape the heat. Their clothes were left on the black sands for there were no men to see them and tapa did not last long if it got wet.

As she was diving into the pool from a shelf on the rocky ledge, Lau-kiele-'ula, one of the companions, saw something moving on the shore. "What's that?" she called. "Who is walking over our clothes?"

She dove into the pool and swam across the shore to where they had left their pa'u. She looked and began to laugh.

"What is it?" asked Nā-pihe-nui from the other side of the pool.

Lau-kiele-'ula called out, "It is a little white dog with a big pink tongue sticking out of its mouth!"

"Dogs are for eating," Nā-pihe-nui said. "Chase it away."

"But this one is so cute," Lau-kiele-'ula said. "Come and see."

Indeed there was a little white dog lying on the pa'u of Nā-pihe-nui, its tongue sticking out of its mouth, and its wide eyes staring unblinkingly at her as she climbed out of the pool and came toward him. The little dog leaped to its feet as she reached down to chase him from her clothes and quivering with excitement the dog licked her hand with its long pink tongue and chased around and around the laughing women until they began to pet him and play with him.

The women played with the little white dog for the rest of the afternoon. He was very quick to learn all the tricks they tried to teach him and indeed sometimes it seemed he was leading them into new ways and Lau-kiele-'ula remarked, "Who is teaching who here?" as the dog initiated them all into a game of fetch-and-carry. No one had ever played with a dog before, for dogs were for eating, like pigs, and no one played with pigs either. The native dog was stupid and lazy and most of the time it was too fat to want to do more than lie in the shade and pant. But the white dog was so amusing and gave them something new to laugh at and talk about and play with that they quickly made him a pet.

The little white dog won their hearts. He leaped around them in great delight and obeyed the call of every one of the companions, but always he showed the greatest affection for Nā-pihe-nui. If she called him, he came at once. If she threw a stick, he ran and brought it back to her. If she felt like petting his soft coat, he was there under her fingertips. From time to time, he would jump up on her and lick her face with his pink tongue and she would push him away, scold him gently, and laugh.

When the shadows were long and the sun was sinking into the waters beyond Lehua island, Nā-pihe-nui and her friends began to walk home.

The little dog went, too.

When the young women settled down to eat their evening meal, the white dog was there, sitting beside Nā-pihe-nui, looking up into her face. From time to time she handed him a bit of food from her hands and he took great care not to hurt her as he took the meat from her fingers.

Polihale saw this dog eating from his daughter's hand and wondered. Through the rest of the meal, the chief watched his daughter and the dog. There was something wrong, he decided. The dog acted like no other dog he had ever seen. Perhaps the dog was under the control of some spirit. Polihale glanced up to the mountains and his stomach cramped as he realized there was no dog-shaped cloud perched on the ridges for the first time in months. And today this strange dog had appeared.

Polihale found his ilāmuku. "I do not like this dog," Polihale said to his constable. "Kill it."

The ilāmuku gathered a few of his trained soldiers and they armed themselves with their slings and stones and clubs. They surrounded Nā-pihe-nui's house and waited until the dog came out. They threw their stones at it but the little dog dodged them all. They tried to club the dog but it twisted and turned and the soldiers missed each time. Then the dog bit the ilāmuku on the ankle and ran up the valley so quickly that the chasing soldiers never saw him again.

A few days later, Polihale heard shouts from the beach. A large red-sailed voyaging canoe had landed, its crew led by a tall young man who was as handsome as any had ever seen. The young chief came to where Polihale awaited him. "Greetings, Chief!" he said. "I have come to ask for your daughter in marriage."

"How do you know my daughter?" Polihale asked, staring at the stranger intently. There was something about the set of his eyes and the shape of his nose that reminded him suddenly of the little white dog and Polihale did not like that memory at all.

"Her fame spreads far and wide, far beyond the confines of Mānā or even of Kaua'i," the stranger said. His tone bordered on the insulting and Polihale knew that he would never give his daughter to this young man.

"Welcome for the time being," Polihale said stiffly. The laws of hospitality demanded no less. "You will have housing and food for you and your crew. I will consult with my priests and my daughter and return to you."

Polihale went immediately to Hōkū-helelei, the kahuna kilokilo. "Look into your calabash," he ordered. "What do you see?"

Hōkū-helelei opened the calabash and breathed on the water, giving it his life force. At the same time, he requested help from his ancestors who had become his guardian spirits. He stared into the depths of the water of life and after a time he replaced the lid of the calabash and looked at his chief. "I see only a cloud, a white dog, a black dog, and a man. Nothing more."

"The cloud I know," said Polihale, looking grimly up the empty ridges where no dog-shaped cloud had been recently. "The little white dog I know, but not the black one. And this man looks like a dog to me."

"Perhaps it is all one," Hōkū-helelei said. "Cloud, dogs, and man, all one, a god who can take shapes at will."

"Perhaps," said Polihale. "We are lost if this is a god. Continue to search your omens and tell me who this being is."

All through that night Hōkū-helelei searched the heavens, watched the clouds, studied the ocean currents, analyzed the faintest breeze that stirred, heard the call of the owl, the rustle of the rat, the squeak of the bat and the high shrill piping of the land shells singing in the valleys. He slept so that his ancestors could talk to him through dreams they would send. At dawn, the kahuna kilokilo returned to the side of his chief.

"He is the god Kū," Hōkū-helelei said.

"How long will my daughter live in the arms of a god?" Polihale replied. "He is not the man for my daughter."

Polihale sent for the young stranger. "You have come here to ask for my daughter in marriage," Polihale said. "I must refuse you. The omens are not good for such a match."

"You're making a mistake," the young chief said, and his voice was a growl with menace deep within it.

"Perhaps," Polihale said, "but there will be no marriage between you two."

"And I tell you there will be," Kū-ʻīlio-loa said. "If you do not permit this marriage,

I shall kill all your people one by one until there will be no one left to protect her except myself."

"You are but one man," Polihale said, although he knew that was not so. But Kū was a cruel god at best. Today there was this demand for a wife. What of tomorrow?

Kū said, "When you have had enough, send Nā-pihe-nui to me." He turned on his heel and stalked away to his canoe and sailed away.

That same day, Polihale saw that the strange cloud had returned to the ridge above. The cloudy shape of a great black dog stretched out of a cave on the mountain side and lolled along the ridge, its misty tongue pink in the late afternoon sun. Polihale realized that this dog with its godly powers would be a very difficult enemy to beat.

The next morning a report came that a lone farmer had been killed by some animal that had torn his throat out with sharp fangs. The next day another man died and another the day after that. Day after day a man died or a woman or a child, until no one went out of doors alone or went heavily armed. But that did little good. The dog went into houses at night to kill while the helpless owner slept.

Day after day, Polihale sent his soldiers to track down the dog. They followed the dog's footprints until the tracks vanished like the dew on the grass after the sun touches them. Setting out guards at night did no good. The dog seemed to know where they were and avoided them easily in the dark. Few saw the dog, yet people continued to die, one after another, one a day.

Polihale said to Hōkū-helelei, "This can't go on any more. What can I do to stop this slaughter?"

"There is only one way," Hōkū-helelei said doubtfully. "Only another god as powerful as Kū can stop him from having his way."

"Which god will help us?" Polihale asked in despair. "And where is this god? How will he get here?"

"Prayers are needed," Hōkū-helelei said, "and sacrifices. You must pray to the gods who are brothers, Kāne and Kanaloa. Only they can stop Kū."

"Collect the sacrifices," Polihale said, "and a place for the prayers. Meanwhile, I must do what I can to protect my people."

Polihale selected a cave in Hā'ele'ele valley in which he could hide all the women and children of his lands. There was a small spring in the cave, enough to last them with care. All the food that could be quickly gathered was given to them. Polihale had the opening of the cave walled up so that not even a little white dog could find a way in. Before the cave, he set a double line of guards armed with sharp spears.

Then Hōkū-helelei led Polihale to the last ravine before the great Nā Pali cliffs begin. Here, on a crude altar of stones, they laid their sacrifices, red sugar cane, red banana, and red i'iwi and 'āpapane birds from the mountains, and red fish from the sea. A cup of 'awa was prepared and placed in a bowl on the altar.

Standing at this altar, Polihale prayed.

> Spirits of my ancestors,
> Stretching into the primeval darkness,
> Help me!
> To Kāne, the eternal one,
> To Kanaloa, the eternal one,
> To the spirits of my ancestors,
> Spirits at the rising and the setting of the sun,
> Stretching back into the eternal darkness of Pō,
> Bring us into light,
> Banish the darkness
> That we may enter into the light.
> Here is my offering of red moano sugar cane,
> And of the moano fish fed on lehua flowers.
> Sacrifices to the gods because we are in trouble.
> To me, Polihale, give divine power,
> Give intelligence,
> Give success.
> O Kāne!
> O Kanaloa!

Climb to the wooded mountains,
Climb to the mountain ridges,
Search the food lands,
Search the marshes,
Look for Kū-ʻīlio-loa,
The white dog,
The black dog,
The man with dog's eyes,
The cloud on the ridges.
Free us from his oppression.
This I promise you,
O Kāne and Kanaloa,
A temple I will build
Here at land's end,
Home for Kāne, the eternal,
Home for Kanaloa, the eternal.
This is the promise of Polihale.
ʻĀmana, my prayer is finished, let it fly free.

The chief and his priest waited for a sign their prayer had been heard. The wind ruffled the surface of the ocean as it always did. The fat heat clouds drifted past as they did each afternoon. Waves hissed across the sand, tumbling shreds of coral and broken sea shells, and sending the sand crabs scuttling to the safety of their tunnels. Nothing had changed.

Then Hōkū-helelei pointed and Polihale looked toward the horizon, toward the long bank of clouds gleaming yellow and pink in the setting sun. Two sea-traveling birds were gliding down the wind toward shore, their five-foot wing spans steady, their eyes intent on their destination.

"The leader is ʻĀ-ʻai-ʻanuhi-a-Kāne," whispered Hōkū-helelei. A large bird, long pointed bill, a tapering body, a black mask across its eyes, white feathers with black primary feathers, for Kāne always showed himself white on one side, black on the other — Kāne had heard and come.

Behind Kāne flew Kaʻupu-hehiʻale, the billow treading albatross, the great white albatross of Kanaloa, a large bird, a white bird sprinkled with black on back, tail and wings — Kanaloa had heard and come.

The great travelers of the seas circled the altar where Polihale and Hōkū-helelei stood. Polihale was no longer alone in his battle against Kū-ʻīlio-loa.

"Good," replied Polihale. "Now we go to battle."

That day, for the first time, the soldiers sighted the large black dog. It seemed to move very slowly, as though it had a great weight on its back. The dog growled and snarled and showed its teeth and the soldiers were still as afraid of it as ever. But Polihale, flanked by his ilāmuku rushed upon the dog and struck it with their clubs. The dog leaped at them but they dodged aside, Polihale striking it on the ribs with his war club as it passed, while the ilāmuku jabbed his spear into the ribs on the other side. The black dog howled.

The soldiers rushed upon it. Hard wooden spears pierced his skin again and again. The heavy clubs broke his bones, his legs, his jaw. In a short time, he lay at the feet of the soldiers, a crushed and bleeding mass. They cut the body of the dog into two pieces and threw the pieces to each side of the valley. Then Hōkū-helelei prayed to Kāne and Kanaloa and the two pieces that had been Kū-ʻīlio-loa turned to stone and stood as a warning to all who entered the valley of Hāʻeleʻele.

Polihale released the women from the cave and went to fulfill his promise to the gods Kāne and Kanaloa. On the slopes of the steep cliff where he had prayed, he built a great temple on five platforms, one above the other, and the houses for the gods were built and prayers and offerings were given at the altar.

Hōkū-helelei named the temple Polihale, for that name means The-Center-of-the-Body, the center of life and the first home of Kāne and Kanaloa on Kauaʻi.

CHRISTINE FAYÉ

ohili lived at the other end of the great Mānā marsh and the brackish lakes that stretched between the limestone sand dunes along the ocean and the black short cliffs of the ridges that flowed from the mountains. He had built his house of thatched pili grass on the high sand dunes of coral and limestone that faced the islands of Niʻihau and Kaʻula like the prow of a huge voyaging canoe. His doorway faced the wind and the ocean and he watched the sun sink to its rest every evening. On one side of his house was a long white beach and on the other were the sheer cliffs of Nā Pali. In front lay the ocean where fish swam in countless numbers and where most days Nohili could be found catching them.

Nohili did not care much for human companionship. Instead he loved dogs and he had nine of them.

People thought he was crazy, for dogs were raised only for food or as sacrifices to the gods. Dogs were fat, lazy, good-for-nothing animals who lay around all day panting in the shade waiting to be fed taro peelings until they got big enough to be eaten themselves. Dogs were voiceless. They could make no sound except for a growl now and then at one another and a yip if they were stepped on. Why would anyone have dogs if they didn't eat them, they asked, for they knew Nohili never ate dog meat or let any dog that belonged to him be killed.

Instead Nohili had collected the nine colors of native dogs. The largest of these was an ʻīlio moʻo, a dog brindled like a lizard's skin. There was an ʻīlio apowai, a gray-brown dog whose eyes and nose were the same color. The ʻīlio peʻelua was striped like a caterpillar and the ʻīlio makue was a solid brown. There was an ʻīlio ʻōlohe, a hairless dog noted for its fierceness and cunning. The four small dogs were the ʻīlio iʻi ʻāʻula, reddish brown like the seaweed; the ʻīlio iʻi keʻokeʻo that was like the whiteness of breaking waves; the ʻīlio iʻi hinahina, the dog that was the gray of the low spreading beach plant; and the ʻīlio iʻi ʻea ʻula, the dog colored like a turtle shell.

When Nohili fished, he tied these dogs to three stakes he had driven deep into the dunes, three dogs to each of the stakes. From the top of this dune the nine dogs would watch Nohili launch his canoe and paddle far out to sea and they waited patiently, for they knew that when he returned Nohili would feed them some of the fresh fish after he had first left an offering at the stone shrine he had built and dedicated to the god of fishermen. Only then would Nohili go to the nearest village to barter for poi or a piece of tapa. The wind, the sea, and the stars he thought of as friends from which he drew his strength and food, unlike the gossip of the villagers which did not offer food and weakened what strength one had. He had the affection of his nine dogs who crowded about him at night to keep him warm and growled to warn him that someone was coming along the path through the dunes. It was a simple life but it suited the fisherman.

One morning, Nohili got out his calabash that held his fishing line and hooks and took it down to the canoe. Then he went to tie up his nine dogs as he usually did. But this morning, as fine and cloudless as a fisherman could ask for, the dogs did not want to be tied up. The big ‘īlio mo‘o growled at Nohili. The ‘īlio pe‘elua fell to the ground, its tail between his legs, and refused to stand up. Nohili had to carry him to the stake and once he was tied up, the ‘īlio pe‘elua whined and cried deep in its throat.

"What's the matter with you all?" Nohili asked. "If I don't go fishing, we'll have nothing to eat tonight. And you all like a full stomach as much as I do."

But the ‘īlio i‘i ke‘oke‘o wasn't taken in by these words and whined and cried and kept just out of reach of Nohili's hands. Nohili finally went to his hut and took down his fishing net. Scooping it up from the center, he draped it over his arm, holding one edge in his hand. Running toward the ‘īlio ke‘oke‘o, he threw the net and the little dog yelped its indignation and surprise as the netting fell over him and caged him so that Nohili could tie him, like the other eight, to the stakes with ropes of pohuehue vine.

It was late when Nohili stepped into his canoe and he was angry with his dogs and so never looked at the sky. He launched the canoe and dipped his paddle into the sea and sped away as fast as he could to make up for lost time. He kept an eye out for flocks of sea-going birds wheeling and diving into a school of fish. He kept his eye out for the telltale flash of silvery fins breaking the ocean surface. Further and further he paddled until the land was out of sight and the sun burned down on his head.

It was hot and no breeze was cooling him as it usually did. There were no birds visible anywhere in the great inverted bowl of the heavens and the ocean itself was flat and he could see deep into the water but there were no fish there.

At last he looked at the clouds. Grimly he saw that a huge front of dark clouds was coming swiftly toward him, bits of clouds torn and tattered from the advancing mass by the wind. It was a storm, coming from the south, and Nohili realized it was a storm unlike one he had ever seen before. No wonder his dogs had whined and tried to keep from being tied up. They were trying to warn him. Dogs knew things people didn't, he should have remembered that.

He dug his paddle deeply into the ocean to spin himself about and headed back toward land as fast as he could. It was not fast enough. Long before he caught a glimpse of land, the storm was upon him. The wind blew waves before it, huge waves, towering green and deadly above his frail canoe. The wind threatened to tear the paddle from his hands. Water washed into his canoe and, holding the paddle grimly in one hand, he bailed it out but the waves kept coming, bigger and bigger, until finally all Nohili could do was hold onto his paddle and try to steer his half submerged canoe into the crest of the waves so that they could not swamp him completely broadside and send him down into the deep quiet green. Hour after hour went by, the wind growing stronger and stronger, the waves larger and larger. Nohili had no idea where he was, no idea where land was. He numbly sat and shivered and tried to keep his canoe pointed into the waves.

Then suddenly the wind died. The clouds roiled past him and the sky above him was brilliant with stars. The ocean calmed and with the cupped palms of his hands, Nohili bailed out the canoe until he rested lightly on the ocean, now as calm and quiet as the sky. Nohili looked at the stars and recognized some of them. Now he knew where he was. Gratefully, he began to paddle in the direction of home.

Far off, he heard a sound he had never heard before, a sound he recognized as made by an animal, no, several animals. He listened as he paddled in the direction of the sound which, luckily for his curiosity, came from the direction of home. Then suddenly without knowing how he had made the connection, he knew he heard his own dogs barking, for they sounded as they looked, the deep throated 'īlio mo'o, the shrill small throated 'īlio i'i. The gods must have taught his voiceless dogs to bark and they were barking to bring him home.

"I'm coming!" he called to his dogs. "Keep making your sounds and I shall come home again!"

But within an hour, the storm returned, the wind now blowing in the opposite direction from before, the waves just as huge and threatening. Nohili found himself plunged into the storm again, his canoe filled with water and he, as before, just as helpless to do anything but try to steer his craft into the waves as hour after hour passed through the long darkness of the night that threatened at any moment to bring him the longer darkness of death.

Nohili no longer knew whether or not he was tired. He had to keep going, had to keep his paddle straining against the sea to guide his canoe over the waves. The wind this time flowed on his back, tearing away the flimsy tapa cloak he had tied over his shoulders. Only the waves, the wind, more wind, more water, and deep inside him the determination to return to his dogs and thank them for trying to warn him. Never again would he ignore their warning, never again.

Finally the storm blew itself out. Nohili awoke, shivering in the night breeze. A half moon shone down on him and the stars twinkled in the sky. He picked out his guiding stars and steered by them back to the shore. Far off, he heard the sound of dogs barking.

"I'm coming!" he cried out. "I'm coming back!"

Soon the roar of surf and a long line of phosphorescent gleam told him he was nearing shore. With the last of his strength, Nohili rode a breaker into shore. He leaped from his boat, felt the sand under his feet, and pulled the canoe up onto the shore out of reach of the hungry waves. Then, his last strength gone, Nohili fell to the sand and slept.

When he awoke Nohili was sore and weary down to the inside of his bones. He struggled to his feet and looked about him. The coastline was not the same. These dunes were not shaped liked the ones he remembered. He climbed to the top of the nearest dune and stood looking down into the marsh of Mānā. Every reed and grass stem had been bent double and sand covered the brackish lakes with a golden film. Across the marsh he could see the ridges of Mānā as they marched down silently from Puʻu-kāpele to dip their feet into the marsh. Along the edge of these ridges there once had been coconut and kukui trees and thatched houses and tall oracle towers in the temples. But now there was little he recognized, only the sand and the ridges.

Nohili hurried to his house but there was nothing where it had once stood. Clean and smooth sand covered the stone paving that once had marked the front of the house. He hurried to where he tethered his dogs. They were not there. He could see the very tip of the stakes he had driven into the sand and around each of the stakes were concentric rings but no dogs.

"Dogs! Dogs!" he called. "Pe'elua, Ke'oke'o! All of you, where are you?"

But no dog answered his call.

He ran to the stakes and at last he heard his dogs barking at him. He laughed with relief. "Where are you?" he called and stopped to listen to their answer.

The dogs stopped barking.

"Where are you?" Nohili called again, unable to hide his confusion and growing fear. "You brought me safely back home. We'll go fishing tomorrow and you'll eat until you can eat no more."

The dogs did not answer and did not come.

Nohili walked forward toward the stakes and the dogs began to bark again. They sounded far away. Nohili stopped again and the dogs fell silent. Nohili looked around, puzzled. Where had they gone to? Why did they bark when he walked but remained silent when he stopped?

Throughout that day, Nohili searched for his dogs. He visited the village where he went to trade fish for poi and the villagers told him of the great storm that had blown away their houses and toppled all the trees and blown down all the oracle towers. But no one could tell him of his dogs. He searched and called but only when he walked on the dunes where he had tied his dogs could he hear them.

That night, Kū-'īlio-loa, Kū-long-dog, the great god in his dog form came to him in a dream and told him what had happened. Kū was a dangerous and blood-thirsty god but he had approved of the care given the dogs by Nohili and so he had given the dogs the ability to bark and they had barked through the terrible storm, as Nohili had heard when he was in the eye of the hurricane. They barked when the storm was over to guide him back to shore, as Nohili had heard over the roar of the surf. It had been Nohili himself who had tied his dogs well to their stakes, three dogs to a stake held with strong rope made of pohuehue vine. The dogs, blown by the wind and frantic with fear for their master, had run around and around their stakes, digging themselves deeper and deeper until now only their voices were left deep within the sand.

Even now people say they have seen a thatched house on the barking sand dunes of Nohili and seen a fisherman sitting outside his house. One by one nine dogs, each of a different color and size, rise up out of the sand and greet the fisherman and lick his hand and curl up around him on an evening when the cold mountain winds blow down from Puʻu-kāpele.

KA LI'ULĀ O MĀNĀ

CHRISTINE FAYÉ

he long voyaging double canoe with its red sails sped across the channel between Niʻihau and Kauaʻi. Kapo-ʻula-kinaʻu sat on the platform connecting the two hulls wearing her long cloak of red feathers speckled with black that gave her her name. She fingered the lei of yellow hala fruit her sisters had made for her that morning before they left Niʻihau.

Before them a new island to explore rose from the ocean. Anticipation of new adventure filled her and she thanked her sister Pele. Kapo, too, had fled the ruins of her homeland, set afire by Pele. Unlike her oldest sister, Nā-maka-o-kahaʻi, she did not seek vengeance. Kapo followed Pele, excited and pleased to see new islands, meet new people, and perhaps find husbands for herself and the covey of sisters who had come with her.

These Kapo-kū-lani sisters stood behind her, clothed in black-flecked red feather capes, holding small feather scepters called kahili in their hands, symbols of the high rank of Kapo-ʻula-kinaʻu. At her feet sat her young brother, Ka-huilao-ka-lani, no longer a boy, not yet a man.

Before them stretched the long beaches of Mānā. Behind the sand dunes they could see marshes filled with reeds and wading birds. On the other side they could see a village surrounded by coconut trees, mulberry shrubs, and sugar cane. Above the cluster of houses rose black cliffs, broken by steep sided valleys that flowed from the mountains. The sun was shining, the clouds were white, the fresh breeze tickled the skin. Kapo-ʻula-kinaʻu laughed as the spray from the breaker swept over them, beading each person on board with a fine salty dew.

Ka-huila laughed with delight. "You are Nā-wahine-makakai, the salt-dewed women," he teased.

The canoe hissed onto the sand. This was new land, seen with new eyes, and already they liked what they saw.

One of Kapo-ʻula-kinaʻu's sisters, whose name was Kapo-kū-lani-moe-haʻuna-iki smilingly said to Kapo, "Already I like this land."

"Do you think you would be happy to remain here?" Kapo-ʻula-kinaʻu asked.

"Oh, yes," Moe-haʻuna replied. "I've just arrived but already I feel at home."

Kapo smiled gently. She alone knew they had come to these islands to stay, that there would be no going back to their homelands. None of the sisters were married and all would need to find husbands and her brother a wife.

Just then, the other sisters called, "Come see what we have found! Something entirely new!"

Kapo and Moe-ha'una joined the young women and inspected the plant they had found. At first Moe-ha'una could only see a koali 'awa vine growing abundantly over the sand, its blue flowers little pieces of the sky fallen to earth. Then she saw that there was another vine with small bright orange stems that had sent down its own roots into the stems of the koali 'awa, a parasite, a vine growing fat from the efforts of another.

"This is a strange thing," Kapo said. "The color of the stem is almost the same as the hala fruit of my lei."

"Indeed it is," Moe-ha'una replied. "Sisters, let's weave a lei for Kapo-'ula-kina'u."

The sisters picked orange vine stems and wove them into a lei po'o which they placed about Kapo's head. This was the first lei of the kauna'oa vine ever made and was a gift from her sisters to Kapo-'ula-kina'u.

By this time a group of people were hurrying toward them from the village on the other side of the marsh. At the head of this welcoming party strode a tall, broad-shouldered man. His arms were long and as strong as the kauila wood spear he carried, and his legs were as sturdy as the crescent-leafed koa trees. His feather cape and helmet were made entirely of the greenish-yellow feathers of the amakihi, a bird found no where else in the world except the mountains of Kaua'i. Behind him hurried his attendants carrying the kahili of his rank and behind them straggled many commoners bearing food and coconut fronds to build a shelter upon the dunes to shade the visitors from the hot afternoon sun.

"Greetings!" the chief called as he came to a halt before Kapo-'ula-kina'u, her young brother, and her many sisters. "I am Limaloa, Chief of Mānā. I welcome you to our land and offer you our hospitality."

"We are glad to be here at Mānā," Kapo replied. "We shall be most happy to share your hospitality if we may ask many questions of you concerning this land of yours."

"I shall answer them willingly," Limaloa replied, "if I may first ask one of you."

"Do so," Kapo answered.

"I know all of Kaua'i," Limaloa said, "for I was born at Hā'ena and have visited every village on the island. But I have not seen any women as beautiful as you before. All of you! Where did you come from? Where is your home?"

Kapo laughed. "We are the daughters of Wahilani and Na-kolo-i-ka-honua," she said, "and we come by way of the mountains." This was true, but it was not the Kaua'i mountains she meant. Kapo had learned in her tumultuous life never to divulge her origins and genealogy to anyone whom she did not know well. She had only just met this handsome chief of Mānā and already there was something about him that troubled her.

She went on. "Listen closely, in order that you may understand." And she chanted.

> O Kapo-kū-lani
> Sisters from the mountains,
> O sisters from the summits,
> Where the waters have their source, come down.
> Come down, O Lau-ka-'ie'ie,
> O Lau-ka-palai, come down.
> Descend, Moe-ha'una-iki.
> Lau-'akolea goes and the upland fills with mists,
> The upland where the mountain flowers are plucked,
> Where the fragrant maile vines are gathered.
> The kauna'oa vine creeps,
> It creeps at Mānā
> Much loved is the trunkless plant.

When Kapo ended her chant, Limaloa was delighted with it and his face lit up with joy. He looked at all the sisters but his eye kept coming back to Moe-ha'una, and the two smiled at each other.

Kapo-'ula-kina'u saw them and thought that here was a possible marriage. But she was disturbed. The last three lines of her chant had caught her by surprise, even as she said them. The last line could also mean "Pity for this vine without a trunk." The vine, she thought, could be a symbol for Limaloa. Why should she have pity? she wondered.

As they ate a welcoming feast under the shelter of woven coconut fronds, Kapo concentrated all her spiritual forces upon this young chief of Mānā, Limaloa. She studied his mind for no thought could escape her, all was as clear as the purest water to her. When she had read all she could, she sighed and looked upon her sister Moe-haʻuna with sorrow.

After the feast, Limaloa invited them to explore his land with him as guide. Together they left an offering at Polihale, where the dead spirits leap off the cliffs to enter the kingdom of the dead. They visited the barking sands and heard the dogs of Nohili barking at their heels as they ran down the dunes. They saw the floating taro fields and counted the water birds as they stalked the edges of the marsh. At dusk, Limaloa took them to Ka-una-lewa to see the mirage, the village of Ka-wahine-o-ka-liʻulā, The-Woman-of-the-Mirage. There were grass houses, coconut trees, and a path of crushed sea shells leading to the largest house, obviously the royal home of the woman of the mirage. But no man or woman could walk down this path unless they had the power of gods, for in reality it was only a mirage, there was nothing there. It fooled the eyes so well most people who saw it thought it was real.

"Who is this woman of the mirage?" Kapo asked.

"Her name is Laie-i-ka-wai," Limaloa said. "After her husband betrayed her with her sister, her parents built her this village until the man who is to be her husband will join her. But, since no one can enter this village for even as you walk toward it, it draws away and then disappears, she will wait forever."

Kapo gazed at the mirage. "Does this woman of the twilight ever appear?" she asked.

"No one has seen her," Limaloa said. "But the legends say she was very beautiful."

"But she is a mirage," Moe-haʻuna laughed. "Can she compare to any of us?"

Limaloa laughed with her. "No," he replied. "You are all beautiful but one more than most." And he looked at her so there was no mistaking his meaning.

Later that evening, Kapo-‘ula-kina‘u took her sister to one side. "Moe-ha‘una, you like Limaloa, don't you."

"Yes," the young woman replied. "And I would not mind staying here as his wife."

"I thought so," Kapo said. "But I am not sure he would be a good husband for you."

"Why not?" Moe-ha‘una asked.

"I have been told all the women of Kaua‘i have rejected him, although no one will say the reason. He is a man who longs to be united with a woman and yet remains without a wife. He falls in love with all women and now with you."

Moe-ha‘una asked, "Who does he love?"

"The woman of the twilight," Kapo said, "although he does't know that yet."

"I have no rival, then," Moe-ha‘una replied, laughing.

Nothing Kapo said would change her sister's mind. Moe-ha‘una wanted to remain on Kaua‘i, wanted to marry Limaloa, chief of Mānā.

Finally Kapo warned her a last time of the woman of the twilight. "I feel he belongs to her," Kapo said, "but I hope I am mistaken. If he does, this is what you must do."

Kapo-‘ula-kina‘u then spoke at great length to Moe-ha‘una but to the young woman it was like giving the wind instructions on how to blow. She hardly listened. She already was dreaming of her future husband.

The following day, Kapo said to Limaloa, "We have enjoyed your hospitality, but it's time for us to leave. However, one of my sisters wishes to remain here."

Limaloa's eyes flamed like a newly caught kukui nut on the torches that brighten the night. "If it is the one I hope it is, I will offer her more than hospitality."

"You would marry her?" Kapo demanded.

Limaloa looked at Moe-ha‘una and smiled at her. "Yes, willingly," he promised.

"Then it shall be so," Kapo-‘ula-kina‘u said. "Take good care of her in every way. She enjoys the beach the most, so make sure she has a home there and that it is surrounded with all the plants that grow in the sand. You won't have to supply her with much food. A full imu every ten days will be enough. She is a quiet woman who delights in chanting and indeed she is best of all of us in that. I've never known her to speak angrily or harshly. You'll find that all her deeds are good. Take care of her."

With that, Kapo sat the two down and covered them with a finely woven makaloa mat while she prayed to the gods for the success of their marriage.

When the ceremony was over, Kapo-'ula-kina'u said, "Now we must go."

Soon she and her entourage were walking down the road to Waimea and the island beyond.

When they reached a little village at the eastern end of the marshes, Ka-huila-o-ka-lani, young brother of Kapo and of Moe-ha'una said, "I already miss my sister. I like being with all my sisters as we travel. You know I love all of you." He burst into tears.

Kapo said, "Let's climb this ridge so we can look back to Mānā where our sister lives now." They climbed up and looking across the marshes to the unending beaches they could see the village where their sister lived.

Kapo-'ula-kina'u chanted a farewell that, carried by the wind, reached her sister's ears.

> O Nā-wahine-makakai,
> Women of the ocean spray,
> On the breadth of Mānā
> Their happy voices are heard in the homes,
> Gentle voices in the calm
> On the shores of Lono-mauna.
> On the great breadth of Wai-o-Lono
> We sing our farewell to you.
> You stay at Mānā,
> We continue on alone
> Even though great difficulties may be encountered.
> Such is the result of dreaming of canoes!
> Moe-ha'una-iki is now a woman of Mānā,
> A woman who walks the shores in the sunshine.
> I will go for a while and return to you,

For here is the dearly beloved sister.
It is your back I see
Kapo-kū-lani-moe-haʻuna-iki.
I call to you, O answer me.

The wind brought one word back, "Farewell!"

Kapo-ʻula-kinaʻu said to her brother Ka-huila-o-ka-lani, "O heavenly chief, be happy for our sister for she has remained behind willingly. Our parents gave all of us the freedom of choice and the spiritual power to overcome any difficulties we meet. We are traveling on and if she wishes to find us, she can do so easily. Don't cry any more, for all of us sooner or later will find homes and remain there. Even you will find a home and stay there as the rest of us go on."

Ka-huila-o-ka-lani smiled. "You're right," he said. "Before we go, I'll give this place a name. It shall be Pokiʻi-kauna, The-Yearning-for-the-Little-Sister."

And from that time to this, the name has remained, even though Kapo-ʻula-kinaʻu and her brother never came that way again.

After her sister had left, Moe-haʻuna went into the sleeping house. "Soon," she told Limaloa, "Kapo will chant a farewell to me. After the chant is over, I'll fall asleep. When I awake we shall be truly man and wife. Guard over me while I sleep so that I am not disturbed."

When Kapo's chant was over, Moe-haʻuna whispered, "Farewell!" and her eyes closed and she fell asleep. Limaloa spread a moelola bedsheet over her. It had been made specially for her at his orders, a sheet of tapa with red and white panels.

Limaloa sat beside his sleeping wife. He watched all that night but at dawn she did not awaken. She did not wake up at all during that day. Three days and nights went by and still she slept.

Limaloa longed for her awakening when they would really become man and wife. He knew he should not touch a sleeping person, for the soul wanders when one sleeps and may be startled by a touch and never return to the body. He could not help himself and reached out to stroke her hair as it fanned out over her pillow.

Moe-haʻuna woke with a start, looking wildly about her, not knowing where she was. Seeing Limaloa, her memory returned and she smiled at him.

"My husband," she said, "why did you awaken me from my sleep? When my older sisters and I slept, we were only awakened with a chant sung by one of our parents."

Limaloa said gently, "You are no longer living with your parents. You are with me."

"Yes," Moe-haʻuna said. "My time for awakening chants is over. Now I am in a land where I am alone."

"You have me," Limaloa said.

Moe-haʻuna said, "Come lie down beside me," and she turned back the moelola.

But as he neared her and prepared to stretch out on the bed, he was overpowered with a force he could never control. Moe-haʻuna-iki watched, first with surprise, then with fear, and finally with sorrow and understanding, as Limaloa's shape blurred and wavered and rippled and begun to fade away. He could not reach the woman whose bed he wanted to share. His soul sped away to search for his great desire, the woman for whom he had born. No wonder all the women of Kauai rejected Limaloa and would never say why. Who could live with a husband who disappeared each time he came near his wife? Who could even explain it to anyone else?

Then Moe-haʻuna remembered what her sister had said that night on the beach near Polihale. She saw a moth fluttering in the rafters of the house and recognized it as the living soul of Limaloa. She rose and took up a small covered gourd and caught the moth and caged it in the gourd, taking care not to injure it.

She walked along the edge of the marsh until she came to Ka-una-lewa. In the moonlight the mirage of Mānā shimmered. Moe-haʻuna walked a little way along the path of seashells that led to the royal house and stopped, uncovered the gourd, and released Limaloa's soul. It fluttered and its form wavered and Limaloa, dressed in his cloak and helmet and armed with his spear, stood beside her.

"You must seek the woman of the mirage as your wife," Moe-haʻuna told him. "You are Limaloa, guardian of the mirage! You belong here."

Moe-haʻuna turned and left Mānā and did not look back. She would never marry again and would become famous as a healer of the sick. If she ever went back to Ka-una-lewa to look at the mirage, no one ever knew it.

Limaloa strode down the village street, his spear of polished kauila wood in his hand, his cloak of amakihi feathers flowing to his heels, and his helmet jutting proudly over his forehead. He went to seek the wife for whom he had been born, Laie-o-ka-wai, The-Woman-of-the-Mirage.

For many centuries, when the moon shone on the nights of Kū, the mirage would appear. First the houses and coconut trees sprang out of the ground. Then Limaloa would step out of his house, his feather cloak falling from his shoulders, his spear in one hand, and stride down the path of seashells to his wife.

This was the mirage of Mānā, the home of Limaloa and his wife, Ka-wahine-o-ka-li'ulā.

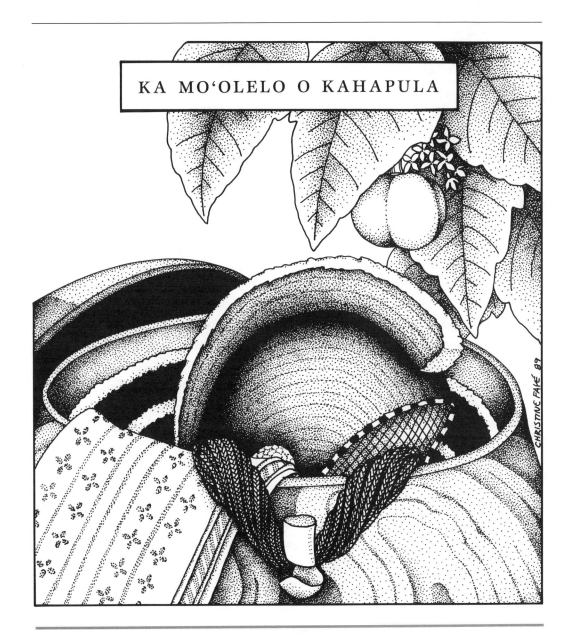

KA MO‘OLELO O KAHAPULA

hese two are lovers," said Kualu-nui-pauku-mokumoku, ruling High Chief of Waimea, pointing accusingly with one outstretched hand at the woman and man kneeling before him. The woman was his wife, the man his chief counselor.

He looked at the crowd of people crowded shoulder to shoulder to hear their ruler's words. He stood at the entrance of Hōwea temple, the heiau built by his grandfather Kane-huna-moku to celebrate the safe arrival of his canoes of settlers, their arrival across the thousands of miles of wild ocean to this land under a sky of strange stars, of steep ravines and rushing waters. With Kane-huna-moku had come his high priest, who was named Hōkū, and his political advisor, who was named Pi'i. Both men had sons named after themselves and these sons had sons and passed on their names, and there lay the source of the present trouble.

Pi'i-mai-wa'a was the kālaimoku, the chief counselor and stood at the right hand of the High Chief. Hōkū-ke'a was now kahuna nui, high priest, and stood at the left hand of the High Chief.

Hōkū-ke'a wanted his own son to become ruler of the island. He had never said so, of course, but over the years since Kualu-nui had become High Chief, a pattern began to emerge, like a black design in a lauhala mat. There were whispered warnings that his chief counselor, the kālaimoku Pi'i, needed watching. The foundation of the chiefdom lay in the ruling chief's complete trust in both his kahuna nui and his kālaimoku. There was no place for suspicion. With each whisper, Kualu-nui had looked and found nothing and he began to wonder.

Kualu-nui had married and had a son. That child was found dead in its bed one morning. He had another son and that one grew, sturdy as a koa tree, for four years before he had slipped, through his own carelessness Hōkū-ke'a said, on the crumbly rocks on the edge of the canyon. Once was the way things were but twice caused the gossip to begin. Kualu-nui was unlucky, they said, he'd never have a son to follow him. Then his wife died, stricken by grief some said, and there were those who wondered if some kahuna anaana had not prayed her to death.

Then Kualu-nui had married again, a young chiefess, like him a descendant of

Kane-huna-moku. Her name was Kahapula. But she, so Hōkū-keʻa whispered, had eyes only for his counselor Piʻi. And Hōkū had brought proof, for he had seen Piʻi leave the sleeping house of Kahapula just before dawn, and there had been several priests who had watched with him.

Now, Kualu-nui stood before his people and condemned his wife and counselor publicly. Kahapula knelt before him, gazing steadily at him. She wore the paʻu she had made, five layers of thin tapa, each of a different color. The outer tapa, the kilohana, she had printed with a design taken from the flowers of the kukui tree. In her hair she had placed a lei of the yellow-green feathers of the ʻāmakihi, the honeycreeper that lived in the chilly forest thousands of feet above them. Beside her stood Piʻi, his malo printed with the same design of kukui flowers. Later the gossips agreed that Kahapula had made the malo. No one else would have dared to use the design of kukui flowers. They wondered at this sign of defiance to the chief.

Kualu-nui looked at them with sorrowful eyes. He leaned on his spear of kauila wood in resignation. Beside him, his beard fluttering in the wind, stood Hōkū-keʻa, kahuna nui in his hour of triumph. His greatest and most feared enemy would soon be gone and he alone would advise the king.

Kualu-nui spoke, pitching his voice to the listening crowd. "You two will go to the valley of Mahaikona and there you will live and there you will stay. Never again will you return to Waimea, never again return to the seashore. Today gather what you will need. Tomorrow you will leave this land."

The crowd dispersed, whispering, chattering, wondering, to return to the daily routine of their lives. Hōkū turned and entered the temple to offer proper prayers to his gods for the success of his plans. Kahapula and Piʻi left to gather clothes, tools, food plants, anything they would need to begin life in a valley far up in the mountains where no one now lived. Mahaikona was the left branch of Waipao valley, the canyon walls towered steeply above the rushing stream, and it was a lonely place. During the day, however, several families came to Kahapula and announced their intention of accompanying their aliʻi wahine, their chiefess, to Mahaikona and several more families came to Piʻi to pledge their support even into exile. No one rested until the last of the kukui nut torches had flared out and Niolopua, god of sleep, had overcome them.

When their supporters had fallen asleep, Piʻi came to Kahapula and said, "Come, he is waiting."

She rose and went with him up the hill to the spring of Wailele. There, Kualu-nui waited for them. Kahapula ran the last few steps to her husband and grasped his hand, her tears washing over it like the gentle rains sweeping the uplands. He held her and touched his nose to hers, then hugged her close. Then he hugged Piʻi and the two men found tears in their eyes.

"Farewell," Kuala-nui said.

"I will come in the nights without moon," Piʻi said, "to this place to bring you news."

"I shall be here," Kualu-nui said. "From tonight, it will be my custom to wander in the night alone."

"I will come as long as I can," Kahapula said.

Kualu-nui, still with his hand in hers, said, "No. Our parting must be final. I could not fool Hōkū long if I continued to see you."

He handed Piʻi a large, hollowed-out, thin-shelled gourd on which the decoration had been carved and dyed as it grew in its field. It nestled in a fiber net which would protect it as it hung from the rafters of its new home in Mahaikona. "When my son is born," Kualu-nui said, "take care of him. While he is growing, teach him all the arts of the warrior and the knowledge he will need to rule. When the time is ready, give him the things in this gourd and send him to me."

"I will," Piʻi promised.

"Guard her well," he said, looking down lovingly at his wife.

"I will," promised Piʻi.

"Return to your rest," Kualu-nui said. Loosing his hand, he whispered, "It will be long before I see you again. But with you lies the future of our people."

"I know," Kahapula said. "Don't be afraid for me or for our son."

Kualu-nui placed a kukui nut into her hand. A little green shoot announced its future growth. "Plant this beside your house. Let its shade cool you, let its nuts flame in the torches to bring you light, and let inamona made from the nuts flavor your poi, and remember me."

She looked back once as she and Pi'i returned to the flood plain of Waimea.

The following day, the exiles picked up their belongings and set off up the Nonopahu ridge, down into Waipao valley, and worked their way up into Mahaikona valley. There, in the following days and months they built houses for themselves, laid out irrigation ditches and taro fields where Pi'i planted the pi'i-ali'i taro his grandfather had brought with him on the voyage of settlement, sweet potato fields were dug and planted. Beside her house, Kahapula planted the kukui nut her husband had given her.

Even as the tree grew, the child within her grew and came forth eagerly into the world, a look of fierce concentration on his face, fists clenched. Kahapula showed her son to Pi'i. "Tell Kualu-nui our son is ready to fight the world," she said. "He is a warrior, our little one."

Soon Pi'i and his wife had a son they named Pi'i-mai-wa'a. He would become the right hand man of his chief and like a shadow Pi'i-mai-wa'a grew up beside the young chief, the son of Kualu-nui-pauku-mokumoku.

Kahapula's son grew tall and strong on the poi made of pi'iali'i taro. He was into everything, mischievous and fearless. Pi'i and his mother taught him well. He knew the intricacies of the kahawai, the laws that govern the use of water, for taro is the foundation of food and without water for all there is no steady source of food. He came to understand how people work best with their own piece of land to farm, willing always to devote one day in ten to farming the chief's land, happy enough, though grumbling, to pay a reasonable tax on the food stuffs they grew. He came to understand that wealth can be measured in the tapa made by women, beaten out in rhythmic cadences day after day and the simple fact that the best cared for wauke trees produced the best tapa. He learned of the plants everyone needed, the lauhala, bananas, pili grass, 'olona for its fibers to make rope. Pi'i took him into other valleys to show him the discontented people who lived under Hōkū-ke'a's yoke and their unkempt farm lands and dry taro fields.

In the shade of Kualu-nui's kukui tree, Pi'i taught the young boy the skills of a warrior. He learned the use of the spear, the club, and the pikoi and the sling. He learned to box, straight-armed, fist-to-fist, and how to hit the opponent's fist in such a way that the opponent's bones broke, not his. He learned to wrestle, learning the holds that would throw an opponent so well that soon there was no one in Mahaikona valley that could beat him at anything.

Eighteen years passed before word came from the lowlands. A runner came to Mahaikona to announce that all young men were to gather at Waimea. The kahuna nui Hōkū-keʻa had announced that the time had come to choose a successor to the aliʻi nui Kualu-nui-pauku-mokumoku, for the High Chief had no children of his own and would choose a young man from his lands to succeed him. In three days the population was to meet at Hōwea for the ceremony.

The young son of Kahapula was eager to go. Kahapula and Piʻi gathered together all the young men of Mahaikona and sent them down to Waimea.

"We will follow tomorrow night," Piʻi told Kahapula. "You will then dress your son in his father's cloak and helmet and he will become the heir of the chiefdom, a son of Kualu-nui who lived. It is for this we gave up our rightful place beside our High Chief."

Kahapula agreed.

But the next day the son of Piʻi-mai-waʻa came running into the valley. "Our chief has been taken by Hōkū-keʻa!" he exclaimed. "He will be the sacrifice before the ceremony!"

"Where is he now? Is he alive?" Kahapula demanded.

"Alive in Hōwea," came the answer.

"What do we do?" Kahapula asked Piʻi.

"Kualu-nui said that only his son's mother could save the boy."

"I gave up my husband, my life as aliʻi wahine, and guarded well my son. I will do more."

"Yes," Piʻi agreed. "That is why Kualu-nui gave you that kukui nut, for it had been given him by the priest in the mountains. Tell her, he said, that when the time comes, Kahapula must take two kukui nuts from the tree, polish them well, and she must go from her home in Mahaikona to the temple where her son is a prisoner juggling these kukui nuts as she goes. If one drops, the boy will die. If she succeeds, the boy will live."

"The gods will give me strength, courage, and patience to do this," Kahapula said. She chose two kukui nuts and polished them. She practiced throwing one up into the air with her left hand, transferring the nut in the right hand to the left and catching the falling nut with her right. After a few minutes of this, she turned to Pi'i. "I am ready," she said.

"I shall go with you," he said. He gathered a crew of men and women and sent them slowly before Kahapula to clear every obstacle from her path. He carried the calabash that contained Kualu-nui's presents to his son and followed Kahapula.

As she went along the path casting up her kukui nuts, Kahapula chanted a song that marked the cadence she needed to keep the nuts flying in the air in rhythm to her walking.

> One day they came in,
> One day remained away.
> Two days they came in,
> Two days remained away.
> Three days they came in,
> Three days remained away. . .

On and on she counted with each step she took. When she reached the mouth of Mahaikona valley, she stopped and chanted:

> This is one, O Hōkū-ke'a.
> Neither side has won the game.
> We clash; the noise reaches the skies.
> I have completed the fiery circle once.

Then she began again, walking toward Hōwea, throwing her kukui nuts into the air from one hand to another. Then after the circle of numbers was reached again, Kahapula stopped again.

That was one, O Hōkū-keʻa.
This is two.
Neither side has won the game.
We clash; the noise reaches the skies.
I have completed the fiery circle twice.

And again she set out, juggling the kukui nuts into the air as she went. Her people went before her clearing the path of stones on which she might stumble, filling in holes, building smooth causeways across the many streams, cutting away low hanging branches that might catch one of the kukui nuts and make it fall from the circle. Slowly the High Chiefess advanced through the heat of noon and into the setting sun that shone in her eyes like the evil glance of the high priest Hōkū-keʻa. But step by step she continued, chanting as she went:

One day they came in,
One day remained away.
Two days they came in,
Two days remained away.
Three days they came in,
Three days remained away.
Four days they came in,
Four days remained away. . .

Up flew the first kukui while the second jumped from one hand to the next, and the empty hand caught the falling kukui as the second was released into the air. The nuts seemed almost to have a life of their own, so regular their flying, a short hop from one hand to another, the long upward flight and fall, the short hop, the high toss, over and over again as the chiefess advanced step by step toward the heiau where her son was a prisoner, waiting execution by the high priest Hōkū.

Her legs trembled and her arms grew tired and heavy and once she almost missed catching the falling kukui nut but she stopped walking for two tosses, breathed deeply, and started up again.

Thus went the ali'i wahine down Waipao valley, over Nonopahu ridge, past the Wailele spring where she had bidden farewell to her husband, and down to the edge of the Waimea river. There she stepped onto a canoe, juggling the kukui nuts as she was oared across to step onto the hot sands.

Here her companions built a shelter of coconut fronds woven together and set out a meal. She could not stop juggling so she was fed, but after a few bites, she refused to eat more and continued her trip. She was so tired, she did not realize she had left the road and was heading back the way she had come but Pi'i walked beside her shoulder and gently moved her back onto the path.

She went along the seashore and then turned inland toward the cliffs, and by the time the moon was rising, she had come to the entrance of Hōwea heiau. Here she stopped and chanted for the last time.

> That was one, that was two,
> That was three, that was four.
> Neither side had won the game.
> We clashed until the noise reached the skies.
> The fifth was almost lost,
> The sixth led on to the seventh,
> The eighth ended with a quick repast.
> The ninth ran off,
> Ran crookedly into a circle.
> Now I have completed the fiery circle ten times.

She caught the kukui nuts and held them still in her hands. "We are here," she said to Pi'i.

"Go in and get him," he said.

Kahapula went into the heiau and found that everyone within had fallen asleep.

Only her son, bound with ropes, was still awake.

He smiled at his mother. "Thank you," he said.

She brushed a hand across his lips to keep them silent and untied his ropes. They went out of the temple together and joined Pi'i, and the three with their followers went to spend the night in a nearby cave. There Pi'i told the young man who his father was and opening the calabash showed him the things within it, presents from his father, proof of his paternity. Then they slept until the coming of day.

By dawn, they could hear people traveling along the road going to the heiau. Kahapula took a malo out of the calabash, one that she herself had made for her husband, this boy's father. It was dyed yellow with 'ōlena and on it she had stamped a pattern of kukui flowers. This she tied around her son's waist. Then she took out the mahaiole, the feathered helmet, and placed it on his head and tied the feather cape around his shoulders.

Then she took out a lei palaoa that had come on the long sea voyage with her grandparents, the hooked pendant made of whale tooth and the cording of braided hair taken from the heads of their ancestors. This she placed around his neck. Only a chief of the highest blood line could wear such an emblem.

At last, Kahapula stepped back. She gestured to Pi'i who stepped forward to hand the young chief a spear of kauila wood.

"A long time ago, I left husband and home," she said to her son, "to give you life. Yesterday, I returned the life to you that Hōkū-ke'a would have taken as sacrifice. Today I send you to your father and you shall give life back to him and to your land. I give you one last gift: your name. It is Ola, Life. Now go and claim your kingdom and your father," Kahapula said.

The young chief smiled at his mother, then greeted his counselor and surrogate father, and motioned to his attendants to rise, for when they heard and seen who he was some had fallen on their knees, while others had fallen on their faces. Then he left the cave and set off for Hōwea, his mother and Pi'i behind him.

Ola came to the door of the temple and two guards crossed their spears across the entrance to stop him from entering. The young chief looked at one, then the other, and the two guards, unnerved, let the spears fall. He entered the heiau and did not notice that a cord stretched across the top of the doorway snapped in two at his coming and fell to the ground.

The young man came to a stop before the High Chief and the high priest Hōkū-keʻa standing on the steps leading to the altar where the young man was to have been sacrificed.

Hōkū-keʻa was rigid with anger. He had seen the cord break and knew only that a chief of unblemished rank could cause that to happen. He saw the regalia worn by the young man and knew suddenly what Kualu-nui-pauku-mokumoku had done. He knew that the High Chief had banished his wife only after he knew she was with child, that he had caused Piʻi to be banished to care for wife and child. Hōkū-keʻa knew he had been tricked.

He was so angry that he forgot where he was. He threw his javelin at the young chief, aiming it at his chest. The youngster brushed aside the javelin as though it were a fly and it landed with a clatter on the stone floor.

"He broke the taboo!" a priest whispered in horror.

Hōkū turned to face the image of his gods that loomed above the altar. He picked up the sacrificial dagger and plunged it into his chest. He slumped forward over the altar, the sacrifice of death he had demanded was himself.

Kualu-nui-pauku-mokumoku greeted his son and brought him onto the steps to stand beside him. "Greetings!" he said. "You bring me back to life by returning my wife and friend to me. And in you, my son, I see the life of our ancestors continue and the life of our land."

Kualu-nui made Ola his heir and successor to the chiefdom and proclaimed that once again Piʻi was the kālaimoku, the trusted counselor of the High Chief. Finally, Kualu-nui greeted his wife. Tears fell from their eyes as they hugged.

During the feast that night, a kahu mele chanted a song telling one and all of the deeds of Kahapula, of her sacrifice, of her exile, of her raising a son, of juggling the kukui nuts, of rescuing her son from Hōwea heiau, of dressing him with the royal insignia, and returning him to his father.

During the feast, Kahapula turned to her husband. "I am going home," she said. "Already I miss my valley of Mahaikona. I like the peace and quiet of my mountain valley. Come and visit me when you can."

Not listening to Kualu-nui's protests, Kahapula returned to sit under her kukui tree, her tapa anvil in front of her, beaters on the right, the dyes and brushes on the left. News from below came to her and from time to time the three men came to visit her, Kualu-nui, High Chief of Kaua'i, Pi'i, kālaimoku and trusted friend, and Ola, her son. She gave them the tapa she had beaten and decorated for them and sent them away again.

And when Pi'i brought her the bones of her husband and told her that Ola was now king, Kahapula hid her husband's bones far up the valley where no one would disturb them and returned to sit under the kukui tree until she finally went to join Kualu-nui-pauku-mokumoku.

KIKI-A-OLA

i‘i-mai-wa‘a was the kālaimoku, the right hand of Ola the High Chief of Waimea. The two had been raised together in the valley of Mahaikona. Ola had been raised to rule, learning the arts of the warrior, the laws of water and land, the care of the people's well-being. Pi‘i-mai-wa‘a had learned of these things, too, and had learned the prayers offered the gods, from whom came all the good and evil that visited the people who lived on the land raising the food crops, the fishermen who caught the fish in the sea, on the reefs, and in the rivers, the bird catchers who plucked the red-yellow, and black feathers of the mountains birds. Pi‘i-mai-wa‘a needed to know all these things for it was his duty to provide his High Chief what he commanded.

Ola found Waimea a difficult place to live. The river opened into the sea, dividing the land in two. To the west stretched a large plain between the cliffs at the feet of the long ridges and a white beach, an ideal place for a village. However, there was no water on this sand flat. Instead the villagers lived on a plain on the east side of the river, hemmed in by cliffs. The fishermen had to climb these cliffs, walk over a dusty plain to Luhi beach which was small and, in times of swells and breakers, dangerous for launching canoes. Across the river from the village the towering cliff of Pali-‘uli dipped its feet into the river. The cliff was perpendicular and no one had found a way to make a path around it. Everyone had to cross the river, either by canoe or by swimming, walk down a bit, then swim across again.

This particular morning, Ola said to Pi‘i, "Let us cross the river. I want to show you something."

Pi‘i ordered a canoe prepared and the two men were paddled across the river. Ola stalked along like an ‘auku‘u, a black-crowned night heron, searching for food on the reefs. "Look at this dirt," he said. He stooped to pick up a handful. "It's good soil. Our people could easily grow gourds, sweet potatoes, and the like here. All we need is water."

"Water is necessary," Pi‘i agreed. "However, this land is higher than the river. Any auwai, irrigation ditch, would have to start further up the river. But there is the problem of Pali-‘uli. How do we get the water around it?"

The two came to Pali-'uli whose black rock face had its feet in the river itself. It towered several hundred feet above their heads. Pi'i signalled the waiting canoe and they were paddled upstream, studying the cliff as they went. On shore again, they paced up the valley, past the junction of the Makaweli stream and Waimea river. Ola and Pi'i studied the terrain.

Finally Ola sighed. "The 'auwai would have to begin above this junction, quite a way above, I think. That is no problem. The problem is the cliff. The ditch there would have to be about four times the height of a man above the river level and be wide enough to have a path so people could easily go from the sand flats to their upland farms on this side of the river."

Pi'i replied, "There is no one of your people who have that kind of knowledge or skill. No one of us could build an auwai like that. No one."

Ola sighed. "Then we can do nothing?"

Pi'i-mai-wa'a replied, "Perhaps we can. The Menehune could build such a ditch."

The Menehune were strange people. They were shorter than Ola's people, with short bowed legs, distended stomachs, and long curly beards. They had come with Ola's grandfather, the first settlers of Kaua'i, but they had always been independent, led by their own High Chief. They were master builders. It seemed that they only needed to run their hands over a rock and they knew exactly how it would fit next to another. They built the walls of temples, they built the irrigation ditches needed to bring water to the wetland taro fields, and they built fishponds. After their coming, they had toured and explored the island and finally had settled in the furthest reaches of Wainiha valley, at a place called La'au-haele-mai, and they cut off almost all contact with the other people of the island.

"Would they help us?" Ola asked.

"We can find out," Pi'i said.

"Then go and ask them," Ola replied. "I'd like to irrigate the sand flats of Waimea."

Ola only had to ask and Pi'i obeyed. That very day he began the journey to La'au-haele-mai. He climbed the paved path from Wai-'awa to Pu'u-kāpele. On the way to Kanaloa-huluhulu, he picked fern fronds and the winged fruit clusters from 'a'ali'i shrubs, making sure he had some of each of the yellow, red, and brown fruits. He wove two head lei which he then carefully packed into a gourd container. Then he struggled across the Alaka'i swamp to Mauna-hinahina, went down the trail that clung to the ridge as an 'ōpihi clings to its wave-washed rock, then climbed upwards through the Wai-niha valley until he reached La'au-haele-mai.

When Pi'i-mai-wa'a reached La'au-haele-mai, he sought out the kahuna nui, the High Priest of the Menehune, the famous Hulu-kua-mauna, the kahuna who glides in the face of the sun. Pi'i stopped at the entrance to the heiau and stood in front of the pūlo'ulo'u, the sticks topped with a ball of white tapa, the taboo sticks that announced that the enclosure behind them was sacred and forbidden to all without business there.

"Where are you?" he called. "I have come."

Hulu-kua-mauna stepped out of the hall where the wooden images were stored. He was, like all his people, short, bow-legged, and bearded. His beard fell below his waist and it was as white as the malo and kihei that he wore.

Pi'i handed Hulu-kua-mauna the two head lei of 'a'ali'i and fern he had woven. Hulu took them, and examined them very closely, the shapes of the fruit bunches, the number of fruit, their color, the leaves. All was in order. There were few indeed who knew that any request to the Menehune had to be accompanied by a lei of 'a'ali'i. This was a sign of important and serious business.

"Who is your chief?" Hulu-kua-mauna asked.

"Ola is my chief," replied Pi'i-mai-wa'a. "He's the great-grandson of the chief in whose canoes your people first came to Kaua'i."

Hulu nodded. This he knew, for long before Pi'i had arrived, his coming was known and the reason for it. Even though he knew, he asked formally, "What is the task?"

"I have come to ask you to build a dam and watercourse at Waimea. We need an auwai built that will bring water from the river around Pali-uli to irrigate the sand flats. It is no easy task for the irrigation water must flow twenty feet above the surface of the river itself. Only the Menehune can do this. This is the message of my chief."

"Wait," Hulu said. "I must ask my chief."

Leaving instructions to give food and shelter to the visitor from Waimea, Hulu-kua-mauna went to his own chief, Papa-enaena.

Papa-enaena was stretched out on a pile of lauhala mats, listening to a storyteller, when Hulu ducked through the low doorway. Papa-enaena sighed. The ringing in his ears had warned him that work was coming. He had been enjoying his leisure very much. He took the lei of 'a'ali'i that Hulu gave him and the two men placed the lei on their heads.

"What is the chore?" Papa-enaena asked sourly.

Hulu replied, "A messenger has come to ask for help. He is Pi'i-mai-wa'a, the kālaimoku of Chief Ola. He says only the Menehune can build an 'auwai around Pali-uli to bring water to the sand flats of Waimea. He says no one in Waimea could do such a thing. Only the Menehune can build this marvel."

Papa-enaena said, "If we build this 'auwai, then the Waimea flats will become fertile and will grow much food. This chief may increase the number of his people by many thousands. Soon there will be so many people that we won't be able to live here in peace."

"We know that in time we must leave this island," Hulu said. "Nothing we do will change that."

"We'll consult with our god Kane-huna-moku," Papa-enaena said. "In the morning we will tell this messenger whether we will grant his wish or not."

Just before dawn, Pi'i-mai-wa'a was led into the presence of the Menehune chief and kahuna nui, both Menehune red eyed from the lack of sleep.

Papa-enaena said, "We have received permission from Kane-huna-moku. We will build the 'auwai for Ola. This work will be done during the month of Makali'i, on the night of Akua, the fourteenth night of our lunar cycle when the moon is almost round."

"What presents and sacrificial offerings need to be made to insure its success?" Pi'i asked.

"Only one sacrifice," Hulu replied. "This project will not begin with a sacrifice of a long black pig, nor a red fish, nor a silver-gray rooster, not even a black coconut."

"This night will be sacred to this water project. No person, be he chief, priest, or commoner, shall light any fire. There shall be no torches lit. No one at all will stir out of their houses at night. No rooster will crow. Pigs and dogs will not roam at will that night nor make a noise. If they do, we will stop our work and return home. What you do with the offender is your business but we suggest you put them to death."

"The only sacrifice we ask is this," Hulu continued. "Your High Chief will lie down on a slab of stone we will place just where the ‘auwai will end and the water will flow over him. He will be asleep so that even when the water begins to flow over him, he will not awake. At that time, just before dawn, the Menehune will leave but no person can see their going except you yourself.

"But as we go, you will give every Menehune a fish all to himself. To prevent arguments, all the fish will be the same. If it is akule, the big-eyed scad fish, then all will have an akule apiece. Which living creature from the waters it is we do not care. When the last of us has passed and been fed by you, you shall return to where Ola sleeps in the water and you will be able to remove him from the water and the Waimea plains will be rich and fertile. If you cannot feed us as we ask, then you will come with us and Ola will die. This is the price we ask to help you. What is your answer?"

"It is not my life," said Pi‘i-mai-wa‘a. "I can't answer for my chief. It is for him to say."

"Indeed it is," replied the Menehune chief. "Go and ask him. If he agrees, send us word and we will come on the night of Mahealani during the month of Māhoe."

Pi‘i-mai-wa‘a returned to Waimea, thinking furiously. He was sure Ola would agree to the conditions set down by the Menehune but it would be he, Pi‘i, who must find a way to feed each and every Menehune that would work on the project. He did not know how many Menehune there would be, thousands perhaps. Could he catch enough fish for them all? To be sure, he would need many more fish than Menehune.

Pi‘i went directly to Ola who said happily, "So, you have come back."

"Yes," was the answer.

"How was Papa-enaena? Will he build our ‘auwai?"

"Yes. He sends his greetings and says the project will be built. They will come three nights after the full moon in the month of Māhoe."

"You do not seem happy at the news," Ola said. "What conditions have they set?"

Pi'i-mai-wa'a told him.

Ola said, "The night will be silent. No one will make noise or go outside their homes that night. No one shall watch the Menehune except you. And I will lie down where the water will flow over me."

"And I," said Pi'i somewhat grimly, "must remain awake and feed all the Menehune so you may live."

"In either case, the water will flow," Ola said. "That is the important thing. Anyway, I trust you, my old friend and companion." Ola touched his friend on the shoulder in appreciation and strode away to consult with his priests on the best layout of the new village that would be built on the irrigated sand flats of Waimea.

Pi'i ordered every fisherman into the ocean. "Catch me the brown-striped moi," he said, "the thread fish that eats seaweed."

The head fisherman said, "They're hard to catch. Moi love the reef edge where the waves surge over the reef. Even though they travel in schools, they're not plentiful."

"Catch the moi, even the little ones, the moi-li'i, and the still growing ones, the pala-moi," Pi'i ordered. "No other fish is as plentiful at this time of year."

Day and night the fishermen went onto the reefs with throwing nets and went out to sea in canoes with long trawling nets. Holding ponds were built and slowly filled with the tawny, brown-striped fish.

As the night approached, Pi'i inspected all the holding ponds. They were full of fish yet Pi'i felt, deep in his bones, that there were not enough of them. How many Menehune were coming? How many moi did he need to save the life of his chief?

Pi'i went into the valley of Mahaikona where he and Ola had grown up and sat beneath the kukui tree of Kahapula. There were times when he needed to return here to gather the strength and peace of mind the soft cool winds and singing waters of the valley brought him. He needed to remember the many lessons he had been taught in the shade of this tree.

In the evening an old man brought him a bowl of poi and a handful of 'ōpae, the fresh water shrimp, and a pinch of red salt. Placing this food on a broad banana leaf, the old man gestured to Pi'i to eat. Pi'i stared at the shrimp and then a warmth of joy began in his toes and spread upwards to his head. Here was fish! Fish in uncountable numbers. There were ʻōpae kuahiwi, the mountain shrimp; ʻōpae kolo, crawling shrimp; there were shrimp that lived in brackish waters, the ʻōpae lōlō. Clawed shrimp, ʻōpae ʻoe haʻa lived in inland streams and taro patches. Every stream from mountain source to sea mouth, every taro patch had shrimp of one kind or another. Every valley had a stream, every valley had men, women and children who could go into the water to search under rocks for shrimp.

Piʻi thanked the old man and ate the shrimp and poi. Then he returned to Waimea and ordered storehouses built on a hillside beside the road to the mountains where the Menehune would pass on their way home. He ordered baskets woven, pools dug that would be fed from a spring, and runners sped through the land with the order that every man, woman, and child must catch their own weight in shrimp.

Soon from every valley, from every stream and taro patch came basket after basket of shrimp. The ponds were full and Pi'i ordered more dug until no one could begin to count the numbers of shrimp.

Then the night before Akua, runners were sent again throughout the lands of Waimea. "Taboo!" they called. "Taboo! On the night of Akua, all will remain in their houses. All pigs and chickens and dogs will be kept indoors so they do not roam and do not make noise. No child shall cry. No man or woman shall call or laugh or cough. No one shall look out their door. Any who breaks the taboo shall die. Taboo! Taboo!" They passed from one end of the land to the other.

The afternoon before Akua began, everyone tied their pigs and dogs inside their houses, put their roosters into large calabashes and clapped the lids on and tied them tightly. Children were ordered to make no noise, no giggle, nor a cry of any sort, or they would die. By dusk everyone was indoors. No fires were lit and darkness covered the land from one end to the other.

Silently the Menehune came with the night. First they brought a large boulder and placed it on the salt plain near the sea. Then they built a tower on it and the Menehune chief Papa-enaena climbed into it to watch the building of the ʻauwai and to give orders.

Then the Menehune placed a flat slab of stone near the cliff of Pali-uli. Piʻi-mai-waʻa and Hulu-kua-mauna led Ola dressed in his yellow feather cloak and yellow feathered helmet and his red malo tied tightly about his waist to this rock and helped him stretch out on it. Then Hulu-kua-mauna uttered a brief prayer and Ola fell asleep, a sleep he knew would either last the night or be the long sleep of death.

The moon of Akua, bright, shining, almost perfectly round, rose into the dark sky and Hina, the woman who lived in the moon, put down her tapa beater to stare in astonishment at the busy land below. On Mokihana ridge a crew of bandy-legged men were pecking holes into the rocks to break them into pieces. A crew of bearded Menehune was hauling these pieces, some of them three feet wide and five feet long, down the ridge and across the river on a dam that had been made that was wide enough to be a path for the carrying of these large rocks. Smaller rocks that could be carried by one man were passed from hand to hand along a double line of pot-bellied men that reached from Mokihana to the work site.

Hina slowed the progress of the moon so she could watch until the work was done. The stone-lined ditch took form, beginning at the dam across the river and down to the black cliff. Around the base of Pali-uli there was now a broad platform, twenty feet above the waters of the river. There was room enough at the top for the ditch and a path. Then, as Hina reluctantly allowed the moon to sink into the west, Papa-enaena, Hulu-kua-maunu and Pi'i-mai-wa'a walked up the 'auwai to the dam. Only a bit of earth stopped the water from flowing into the 'auwai to irrigate the sand flats of Waimea. The three men prayed to their gods and when the prayers had been said with no faults, Papa-enaena took a digging stick and broke open the bit of earth and the water began to flow down the 'auwai.

The three men followed the water as it worked its way down the ditch. Here and there, the water tried to escape and leak back into the river but Papa-enaena only had to gesture and the Menehune engineers fixed the leak and the water continued down the 'auwai.

They walked along the broad path and Pi'i-mai-wa'a stood a moment looking down twenty feet to the surface of the river and then up at the cliff then at the water flowing past in the ditch. They passed Pali-uli and the 'auwai came to an abrupt end. Here the water spurted out of the 'auwai and tumbled down on the still form of High Chief Ola asleep on the slab of stone.

"Our work is ended," Papa-enaena said. "You didn't ask us to create the entire irrigation system, just the 'auwai around the cliff."

"That is so," Pi'i replied. "Only the Menehune could build such an 'auwai but now we can build a village here on the plains of Waimea, watered by the Menehune's ditch."

"We must return to our homes," the leader of the Menehune said. "We're tired. And hungry."

"There is food for you along the way," Pi'i-mai-wa'a replied. He hurried away to the hill where the moi were stored. As each Menehune workman passed him, he handed the man a moi all of his own. As Menehune after Menehune passed, the supply of moi grew less and less. At last Pi'i-mai-wa'a served the last of the moi. But standing in front of him, their hands empty, were Papa-enaena and his kahuna Hulu-kua-mauna.

"There is not enough," the Menehune chief said. He ordered all his subjects to return and replace the moi they had taken. "There is still something else," Pi'i said grimly and led the way to another hill that was now covered with baskets full of fresh water shrimp. Once again, as each Menehune passed him, Pi'i handed him a shrimp. This time, even Papa-enaena and Hulu-kua-mauna received a shrimp of their own. The bargain had been kept. The 'auwai was built and Ola would live.

As the Menehune climbed up the road into the mountains they shouted and yelled and laughed, breaking the taboo of the night of Akua. They yelled so loudly that their noise frightened the birds on Oahu and they climbed into the sky in a swirling frightened mass, wheeling about, not understanding what the noise was.

Pi'i-mai-wa'a rushed back to the 'auwai. His High Chief still slept there with the water spurting over him. Pi'i took his chief's hand and lifted him into a sitting position. Ola awoke and, feeling the water splashing on his back, laughed.

"Now we shall have a village!" he said.

Ola ordered his people to dig the irrigation ditches from the Menehune's 'auwai. They dug new taro fields and lined them with stones and planted the edge with bananas and sugar cane. They planted wauke, the mulberry trees whose bark was beaten into tapa for the clothes they wore, and gourd vines that gave them containers for water, food, and all their possessions. Everything grew well in the fertile soil, the hot sun, and the spurting water.

This great ditch built by the Menehune around the base of Pali-uli was named Kiki-a-Ola, The-Spurting-Water-of-Ola.

KA‑IKI‑PA‘A‑NANEA

CHRISTINE FAYE 91

A thousand years ago, there was a large sports field at Wai-lele on the east bank of the Waimea river surrounded by a low stone wall where spectators came to watch feats of physical strength, cheer on their favorites with yells and huge bets, applaud the winners, and jeer the losers. When a certain young chief became the Ruling Chief, the people of Waimea were at first very pleased. The chief was tall, broad, and very strong. His arms were like the branches of a koa and his thighs were like the trunks of the kauila. He enjoyed sports and often ordered public exhibitions of the three games he loved most.

First there was honuhonu. In this game, each of the two contestants sat on the ground facing each other. Locking their feet together, hooking toes around insteps, they tried to throw each other over. Honuhonu was a sport that demands strong toes and strong thighs and no one on Kaua'i had stronger toes or stronger thighs than the young Waimea High Chief and he always won.

The second sport was hakoko. The two combatants stood face to face, grimacing wildly to try to scare or anger the other. Then, on a signal, they tried to seize hold of each other and struggled to trip the other with the use of their feet. The one who was thrown to the ground was the loser. Hakoko calls for good balance, strong arms, and great agility with the use of legs and feet. The young Waimea chief was a skilled athlete and he always won his bouts.

The third and most dangerous was mokomoko. The two challengers would beat and pummel each other with their fists and each boxer sought to receive his opponent's blow with his own fist. Mokomoko was a sport that could cause great misery to the players for it was easy to end up with a broken arm, an eye put out, or teeth knocked out. The boxer who first fell to the ground was the loser. It was a sport that called for strong arms and fists like the head of an axe, and for a long, long time no one had ever beaten the Waimea chief at this sport.

He was called "The-champion-of-Kaua'i" from one end of the island to the other. But, in all too short a time, his name among his people became Ka-iki-pa'a-nanea, The-trifler-in-petty-amusements, for he was not interested in the welfare of his people or in his religious duties. He always demanded a full crowd of spectators at all sports events which were held often and the land and gods were neglected and everyone but the chief began to suffer.

After a day of wrestling and boxing, the chief enjoyed matching wits in asking and answering riddles. In the beginning, he lost some of these contests but, angry at losing, he composed a two-part riddle no one could answer. The poor man who could not answer this riddle was thrown into an imu filled with hot stones and so died.

No one on Kaua'i would challenge Ka-iki-pa'a-nanea willingly, for even if they won at hakoko or honuhonu or mokomoko, they had to try to answer the two-part riddle and were put to death. Everyone eagerly awaited any malihini, newcomer, who came unwary to Ka-iki's court. The malihini was immediately challenged to enter the sports arena. If by chance the malihini won the game of honuhonu, he was immediately challenged to try a bout of hakoko. Ka-iki usually won that, but if by chance the newcomer won that bout, he found himself in a game of mokomoko. Of course, if the malihini felled the chief with his fists, he was invited to an evening of riddles.

Ka-iki-pa'a-nanea enjoyed these games and if no challenger came from overseas, he would order his two attendants, Ke-au-miki and Ke-au-kā, to find him someone to play honuhonu, hakoko, or mokomoko with him, or someone to match riddles with him. As that always ended with the unwilling challenger thrown into the imu and baked, there was no one on Kaua'i who was not afraid of what could happen to him. Everyone hated and feared Ka-iki's games. They hated and feared the two attendants, Ke-au-miki and Ke-au-kā, but the people dared not say a word to either of them, for anyone who did so quickly found himself before Ka-iki in the center of the sports arena at Wai-lele.

It was Kūkae-ā who was taunted, spat at, had stones thrown at him and, if he was not careful, got beaten up.

Kūkae-ā was the Ruling Chief's personal attendant. Since Ka-iki-pa'a-nanea was very superstitious and was afraid a sorcerer might obtain a bit of his living body to use in his enchantments to pray him to death, Kūkae-ā had to collect every hair that fell from the chief's body, every paring of finger and toe nails, and every liquid or solid that came from the chief and hide them where no one could find them. Since Kūkae-ā also prepared the imu for the riddling contests, he usually burned these things in the imu along with the victim. Because of his duties and because he never had time to bathe, there was always a disagreeable odor clinging to him. People avoided him or stood upwind of him. Ka-iki-pa'a-nanea would let his attendant only wear his cast off clothes, so he was always dressed in rags. He ate the leftover food from Ka-iki's meal, all the gristle and fat the Ruling Chief would not eat. He could never leave the side of the chief day or night and always hovered nearby, waiting to snatch up any living substance that might fall. It was known that Ka-iki never spoke to him and ignored him and would never listen to him if he did speak, so the people of Kaua'i could express their dislike for their Ruling Chief directly to Kūkae-ā. There was no one more reviled or miserable on all Kaua'i.

Ka-iki-pa'a-nanea was almost completely contented with his life. Ke-au-miki and Ke-au-kā always found him someone to wrestle with when he got bored. They always found someone to play the deadly game of riddling with him. All in all, the Ruling Chief was very pleased with himself and his life. There was only one thing wrong.

He was without a wife.

One day Ke-au-miki and Ke-au-kā sailed away in a red-sailed canoe to search for a wife for their Ruling Chief. When they arrived off the shore of Waikiki beach on Oahu, they saw a young woman surf riding who was very pleasant to look upon. She was without blemish and was so beautiful that she could only be compared to the beauty of the full moon. When Ke-au-miki and Ke-au-kā first saw her they were so attracted by her good looks that they could not keep their eyes from her. Therefore they sailed next to her, pulled her from her surfboard into their canoe, and took her off to Kaua'i to Ka-iki-pa'a-nanea.

They did not know that this lovely woman was Mākolea and that she was the wife of Ke-paka-'ili-'ula, a chief of highest rank and a renowned warrior and athlete. These two had left their lands on Hawai'i to visit the famed places on each island. On Oahu they were the guests of Ka-kuhi-hewa, the Ruling Chief, and on this day, Mākolea had gone to slide on the giant waves of Lehua-wehe.

Mākolea's attendants swam to shore to tell Ke-paka-'ili-'ula his wife had been kidnapped and they were sure she was to become a sacrifice on some altar or another. She might already be dead.

Ke-paka consulted with a kahuna kilokilo, a man skilled in reading the events of man in the happenings of nature. The kahuna killed a rooster, a dog, and a fish, and studied their intestines. Then he said, "No, Mākolea is not dead. She has been taken by Ke-au-miki and Ke-au-kā, the attendants of the High Chief of Kaua'i, Ka-iki-pa'a-nanea." That same day, Ke-paka-'ili-'ula asked the Ruling Chief of Oahu for a canoe to make the voyage.

Ka-kuhi-hewa offered him a double canoe and some warriors.

Ke-paka refused to take the soldiers, saying, "I don't want to travel in state, for my wife has been taken away from me secretly, so I want to travel in secret. Since Ka-iki-pa'a-nanea has come and taken my wife like a thief, I, too, will adopt the same course. I only want a small canoe."

Ka-kuhi-hewa therefore gave him the small canoe he requested.

Ke-paka sailed for Kaua'i that very evening and on the morning of the next day he reached Luhi beach on the east side of the Waimea river mouth. As soon as he landed he took his canoe and broke it into pieces and left them on the shore. He would not need a canoe again until he had found Mākolea and could return to Oahu with the full honors due to their rank, freely given by the Ruling Chief of Kaua'i whoever he or she might be then.

He climbed up the hill to the flat of Hipo and went to the first chiefly house he saw. This was the home of Chief Ka-una-lewa, a wealthy and honored man. When Ka-una-lewa saw the royal appearance of Ke-paka, he invited him to be his guest. By the next day, the men had become friends. Ka-una-lewa promised, "Whatever you request of me I will grant it."

On the third day, the voices of the people were heard shouting and yelling below them at Wai-lele.

Going to the edge of the cliff and looking down, Ke-paka asked his friend, "Why are those people gathered in that place and what's the reason for their shouting?"

Ka-una-lewa replied, "It's our High Chief Ka-iki-pa'a-nanea. He's brought a chiefess from Oahu to be his wife but she's told him she'll only be his if there's no one on Kaua'i who can best him. Now they're playing honuhonu. After that there will be wrestling and boxing. Then they'll give and answer riddles. No one can beat him. He's always the winner. Someone must have been thrown just now and Ka-iki always likes great shouting for the winner."

Ke-paka, asked, "Can we visit this place?"

His friend answered, "It might be dangerous for you, but why not?"

They went to the sports arena of Wai-lele. There they found Ka-iki-pa'a-nanea under a shelter of woven coconut fronds lying on a platform of lauhala mats being wiped down by Kūkae-ā. Beside him sat the woman from Oahu. Mākolea sat as far from the chief and his smelly attendant as she could. She stared ahead of her and her eyes only flickered once as the people catching sight of Ke-paka-'ili-'ula shouted their admiration, for the newcomer was just as huge as their chief and was even better looking. Some of the women began to weep out of pity for him, for they were sure he would be killed by Ka-iki.

When Ka-iki saw Ke-paka, he called out to him. "Hello, newcomer, come this way and join in the games with the old-timer. We're just about to play honuhonu."

Ke-paka said, "I've never played honuhonu. I know nothing about it."

Ka-iki replied, "If you don't know that game, how about a game of hakoko?"

"I don't know that game either."

"Let's go a bout of mokomoko then."

"Yes, I have played that game," Ke-paka answered. "I've never been declared an expert at it, but I'm willing to play mokomoko with the old-timer."

At this, Ka-iki, a happy grin stretched across his lips, led the newcomer to the center of the arena. The men took their stances facing each other. Ka-iki asked his opponent, "Who shall have the first chance, the old-timer or the newcomer?"

The stranger answered, "Let the old-timer have the first chance and the newcomer the last."

Ka-iki immediately struck at Ke-paka who was expecting, as was usual, to trade insults and boasts before beginning to spar. The blow hit the newcomer on the shoulder, causing him to stagger back and almost fall to the ground. Ke-paka, with one great effort, steadied himself and in a moment he had resumed his stance before his enemy.

Grimly the newcomer struck Ka-iki, hitting him squarely fist to fist with incredible force. The crack of a breaking arm bone resounded and Ka-iki, his feet twisting together, fell to the ground, wet his malo, and became unconscious. He looked as though he were nearly dead.

The spectators shouted and yelled and reminded each other over and over of the great strength exhibited by Ke-paka. Then they remembered the two riddles of Ka-iki and they fell silent in sorrow for the champion for they knew he could not escape the riddles.

Having been unconscious for some time, Ka-iki came to and said boastingly, "Say, but that was a good blow! You've made the game worthwhile at last!"

Ke-au-miki and Ke-au-kā carried their chief away to set his broken arm. With a brief glance at Mākolea, Ke-paka and his friend Ka-una-lewa went home.

Three days after this encounter, Ka-iki sent his servant Kūkae-ā on a circuit of the island to notify everybody to come together at the chief's sports arena to answer the chief's riddles. In each district, Kūkae-ā called out:

"In four day's time, all the people are commanded to come to the sports arena at Wai-lele and solve our chief's riddles. He who answers them correctly will be saved but he who answers wrongly will be thrown to his death in the oven of hot stones. No man, woman, child, or those weak from old age shall remain at home. If anyone remains at home on that day, his house shall be burned down and the chief's punishment shall be meted out to him and his family from the parents to the children, to all relations to the last connection and even to friends."

At the end of the day, Kūkae-ā came to the house of Ka-una-lewa and called out the chief's proclamation at the top of his voice.

When Ke-paka-'ili-'ula heard this call, he asked his friend, "Who's the man who's yelling like that?"

Ka-una-lewa replied, "It's only Kūkae-ā, the personal servant of Ka-iki-pa'a-nanea."

"Call to him and ask him to come in," Ke-paka said.

"But he's unfit to be seen," protested Ka-una-lewa. "He smells bad."

Ke-paka, however, insisted, telling his friend, "Call him to come here for I'd like to talk to him."

Because of the promise he had made his new friend, Ka-una-lewa reluctantly called out to Kūkae-ā to enter his house. Kūkae-ā turned toward them but at some distance away, he stopped and said, "It is not proper for me to come any nearer, for I am not fit for your company."

Ke-paka, however, walked up to him and said, "Open your mouth. You must be thirsty after your journey." Kūkae-ā opened his mouth and Ke-paka poured water from a gourd bottle into his mouth and over his body. Then Ke-paka led him to the sea and told him to scrub himself with wet sand and bathe in the ocean to be rid of the foul odor of his body.

Then Ke-paka gave him a new length of tapa cloth which the surprised man quickly tied into a malo. Ke-paka led the amazed Kūkae-ā into the eating house and set before him bowls filled with fresh food that no one's fingers had as yet touched and invited him to eat. Kūkae-ā sat down and ate quickly until he could eat no more.

When he finished his meal, he turned and said to Ke-paka, "What shall I give you as payment for this great kindness? I've lived from my birth to this day with my chief and have often made the rounds of Kaua'i but no one has ever given me a new malo or fresh food to eat. Finally I've found out that poi and meat are indeed pleasant to the taste."

"I don't want payment," Ke-paka said.

Kūkae-ā laughed. "You should, for if I don't help you, you'll die. You're the first person to beat Ka-iki at mokomoko since he was a child and because of that, you'll die in the hot oven unless you answer his riddles correctly. Therefore I could give you in return for your goodness the answer to the chief's riddles. I was there, unseen, unheard, and unnoticed as usual, when he made them up. I am the only person that knows the answers."

Kūkae-ā remained silent for a time. Ke-paka could see he was making up his mind to something and did not rush him. At last, the man straightened up his back and said,

"However, before I tell you riddles and answers, you must promise to help all of us on this island to be rid of this monster."

"Gladly," Ke-paka said. "Tell me what your plan is and what are the riddles and their answers."

Kūkae-ā told Ke-paka the answers to the Ruling Chief's riddles and what to do after he had answered them correctly.

Ke-paka looked steadily into Kūkae-ā's eyes and found only truth there.

Ke-paka said, "You go home now, but whenever you get hungry, come here and have something to eat."

On the fourth day after this meeting, the people of Kaua'i gathered at the chief's arena at Wai-lele. Ke-paka and his friend Ka-una-lewa came also.

Beneath the woven ceiling of coconut fronds, Ka-iki-pa'a-nanea reclined on a pile of lauhala mats, his healing arm held carefully across his chest. Mākolea sat behind him, idly playing with a kahili wand of polished wood tufted with a profusion of colored feathers. The chief's two guardians, Ke-au-miki and Ke-au-kā sat nearby, ready to offer him a cup of 'awa. The chief was already under the influence of the narcotic drink. To one side of the shed, Kūkae-ā was tending to an imu long enough for a man, a fierce fire heating the stones to a shiny red.

When Ka-iki saw Ke-paka, he called out. "Let the newcomer sit here," he said, pointing to the mat in front of him.

As soon as Ke-paka sat down, the Ruling Chief said, "Will the newcomer join in the fun?"

"What's the fun for today?" Ke-paka asked innocently.

"Today's sport consists in posing and answering riddles. Whoever answers my two riddles correctly will be saved from the oven of heated stone but if either answer is wrong, he shall be thrown to his death in the oven. I want the newcomer to understand. If you give me the right answers you will indeed live, but if you fail I shall kill you." Ka-iki smirked with anticipated glee. His enemy would soon feel the vengeance of Ka-iki-pa'a-nanea.

Ke-paka said loudly so everyone in the arena could hear him. "Let the chief pose his riddles so that the people will know what they are. If I do not answer correctly, the punishment is already known. It will be death in the oven."

The High Chief said, "Here is the first half of my riddle.

Ka'i a puni,
Ka'i a lalo,
Koe koena.

Plaited all around,
Plaited to the bottom,
Leaving an opening."

Ke-paka glanced at the oven and saw that the stones had turned deep red. Ka-iki waited impatiently for the newcomer to speak and drank off his bowl of 'awa and flung the bowl away over his shoulder. The two guardians smiled broadly. Mākolea sat motionless, her kahili aimed like a small spear at the back of her kidnapper. Then, unnoticed by all except the malihini chief, Kūkae-ā nodded.

Then Ke-paka-'ili-'ula gave the answer to the first riddle. "The answer is a house. It is thatched all around, except for the doorway. A house is thatched on all four of its walls. A house is thatched from the ridge of the roof to the ground. Only the door is left as an opening. Am I right?"

Ka-iki-pa'a-nanea was dumbfounded. No one had ever guessed his riddle before. This was indeed a challenge, but one he was prepared for. "Yes, you've given the right answer to my riddle. Now here is the second to be answered.

O kanaka i kū,
O kanaka i moe,
O kanaka i pelupelu'ia.

The men that stand,
The men that lie down,
The men that are folded."

Ke-paka looked at the oven and saw Kūkae-ā throwing the stones to one side, so he answered the second riddle. "The answer is also a house. The men that stand are the posts set into the ground. The men that lie down are the beams that connect the posts, and the men that are folded are the pili grasses bent in two to make the bundles that thatch the house. Am I right?"

At this Ka-iki angrily demanded, "Who has given you the answers to my riddles?" He had never thought what would happen if someone actually answered his riddles correctly.

Ke-paka jumped to his feet and lifted the astonished High Chief over his head. "If the answers are correctly given, then it is the chief who will die," he said.

Ka-iki-pa'a-nanea screamed at his attendants and to all his people, "Help me!"

The spectators watched, hardly daring to breathe. Only Ke-au-miki and Ke-au-kā rose to their feet but Mākolea jabbed them as hard as she could on the kneecaps with the sharp point of her kahili and they fell howling onto the mat.

Ke-paka ran forward to the imu with the chief high overhead and tossed him onto the fiery stones. Kūkae-ā just as quickly piled red hot stones on top of him.

A few of Ka-iki-pa'a-nanea's soldiers rushed at Ke-paka in an attempt to kill him, Ka-una-lewa tossed his friend a war club and, his own short spear and dagger in hand, joined in the fracas. Mākolea joined her husband, ready to use her kahili as club or spear or dagger. Kūkae-ā stepped forward, a huge pole in hand. The few defenders of Ka-iki were quickly broken like twigs.

Ke-paka-'ili-'ula led Ka-una-lewa to the center of the sports arena and in a loud voice so everyone at the edges of the crowd could hear him, said, "Ka-una-lewa shall be the Ruling Chief of the whole of Kaua'i. He shall be the chief of the things above it and the things below it, the things in the uplands and in the lowlands, the things that are cooked and uncooked. He shall be the ruler of the land and Kūkae-ā shall be the right arm of the chief, his kālaimoku."

The people of Kaua'i shouted their approval. Lesser chiefs crowded around to pledge their loyalty to their new ruler. Warriors began mock battles if they thought the new Ruling Chief was looking to demonstrate their worth as soldiers. Farmers thought of ways to remind their new leader of their worth and food soon appeared, platters of pork and dog, bowls of poi, baked sweet potatoes, salted fish, seaweed, and a feast began. Ke-paka and his wife Mākolea were led to seats of honor beside the new ruler and his chief advisor. Flutes whistled, rattles shook, bamboo wands clicked, voices lifted in song, and dancing began. Only as the sun the next morning stared down in astonishment at the celebration did people begin to return to their homes and fall asleep.

NĀ MAI‘A O MANUAHI

ake way! Make way!" The sound of shouting voices bounced from cliff to cliff along the lower Hanapēpē valley.

Farmers ran to hide their corms of taro. Bird catchers hid their bunches of red and yellow feathers. Trainers of fighting cocks grabbed their roosters, popped them into a calabash, and slammed down the lids. Tapa beaters tapped out a message on their anvils: "'Ānunu is coming!"

'Imi looked up from his work, making a waterway from Manu-ahi stream to his banana patch which lay under Hōlei ridge that separates Manu-ahi from Kō-'ula valleys. His full name was Ke-kanaka-'i'imi-'ike, The-man-constantly-seeking-knowledge, for at this time Kaua'i was a vast unknown land. Most people were content to huddle together in deep valleys, feeling protected by the cliffs, but 'Imi rambled here and there, looking into deep canyons no one had seen before except for strange people who hid deep in the mountains and spoke in shrill, chittering voices like the small birds that flitted through the lehua trees. These people lived on the banana tree. They ate the fruit, they clothed themselves with the leaves, and braided rope from its trunk. 'Imi, because he always went alone, slowly made friends with these people and from them he learned how to plant and take care of the trees. As he discovered new valleys, 'Imi also discovered new kinds of bananas growing wild. These he collected and brought to his farm.

'Imi had chosen to live where the Hanapēpē valley splits in two. On the right hand, named after a wild red sugar cane, was Kō-'ula. On the left, named after the 'alae bird from whom Maui had learned the secret of fire, was Manu-ahi. Where these two streams joined, there was a cliff and below the cliff was a spring of water. Here 'Imi built a house for himself. As the days went by, he gathered the different bananas and planted them in patches up and down Manu-ahi valley. There was the mai'a-'ū, the snub-nosed banana whose yellow fruit was only edible when it was cooked. He grew the mai'a 'ele'ele, the banana with a black trunk and orange colored fruit. He transplanted the mai'a hāpai whose small, yellow, sweet fruit grew hidden within the trunk of the tree itself.

Day after day 'Imi looked for new kinds of bananas and tilled those he had transplanted into Manu-ahi. Time after time he delivered hands of bananas to the konohiki chief of Hanapēpē, whose name was 'Ānunu, who in turn delivered some of the bananas to his high chief, the great Kū-alu-nui-kini-akua. In return, 'Imi received taro and fish and, all in all, thought he had a very pleasant life indeed.

"Make way! Make way!" echoed the voices from the cliffs. A cortege of six men appeared, two leading the way shouting and four men carrying a manele, a net hammock slung between two shoulder beams, and in the manele, swaying gently from side to side, rode the konohiki chief, 'Ānunu.

He liked to ride about his lands frequently, inspecting all the taro patches and sweet potato fields, fingering the tapa and lauhala mats, and visiting the banana patches of 'Imi. 'Ānunu loved bananas, for his chief, the great Kū-alu-nui-kini-akua, enjoyed a pleasing mouthful of wild banana after drinking his 'awa and always looked more kindly upon 'Ānunu after such a present. 'Ānunu insisted upon the finest, lushest, biggest, most succulent foodstuffs and tapa and mats grown or made by his farmers, for he was a greedy man and liked nothing but the best for himself. And so, of course, everyone in Hanapēpē feared him and hid everything they could from him.

'Ānunu ordered his manele carriers to stop beside 'Imi. The carriers were glad to rest, for the trip was long and 'Ānunu was very heavy. 'Ānunu remained in his manele and looked about 'Imi's banana patch with interest. Standing in the middle of the patch were two kinds of bananas he'd never seen before. One tree had a tall yellow-green trunk and its huge bunch of yellow-skinned fruit not only pointed upward instead of down, but was so big and heavy the bunch nearly touched the ground. It stood proud and tall and strong. The other banana tree had a bashful air, seeming to shrink in on itself, trying not to call attention to its trunk of green, purple, and pink. This shy banana's fruit was also ripe and heavy and 'Ānunu's mouth watered.

"You have found new bananas," 'Ānunu said to 'Imi. "Congratulations! I shall expect these two bunches at my compound tomorrow afternoon."

'Imi was too surprised to object. He, too, had never seen these trees before. They were completely strange. 'Ānunu waved his men on, and closed his eyes and thought delicious thoughts of the feast of bananas to come and how he would be rewarded by his High Chief.

As his chief disappeared up Kō-ula, ‘Imi sighed. He went to look closely at these strange trees. The more he looked, the more he knew he'd had nothing to do with their being in his patch and he began to suspect what they were.

"If I'm right," he murmured to them, "you are kupua of some kind, demi-gods of some sort. Tomorrow I must take two bunches of bananas to ‘Ānunu but to do that I must cut down the trunk and that will be the end of you."

Sighing unhappily, ‘Imi spent the rest of the day wandering up and down Manu-ahi, hoping to find two bunches of bananas that were as finely colored, as large and tasty looking as the two that stood in his patch. But no other tree that was bearing fruit would suit his purpose. So, he decided, he would simply send the best he had and hope that ‘Ānunu wouldn't know the difference. He would not cut those two new trees down. No matter what, he would not.

That night, ‘Imi stretched unhappily on his bed. Just then, a voice, just outside his door, called "‘Imi! Come out and talk to us."

‘Imi poked his head out and saw two tall strangers, who looked almost exactly alike, except one was a woman and the other was a man.

"My name is Polapola," the man said. "This is my sister Melemele. We are kupua, two of the demi-gods that live in Ka-honu-moku."

‘Imi knew Ka-honu-moku was the home of the gods, a land hidden behind the clouds during the day. He stared at Polapola with eyes as big as the owl.

"You know that the stars are the eyes of the kupua who live in Ka-honu-moku," Polapola said. "At night, my sister and I look down on the earth below. During the night, we take the shapes of people, but during the day we have the shapes of banana trees. So, of course, we were very interested in your collection of bananas. Last night we decided to visit you, and so we climbed into our canoe and paddled down the pathway of the stars and came ashore at Hanapēpē bay. For the rest of the night we strolled along the banks of the river and just before dawn we arrived at your farm. But it was almost daylight and so we went into the grove of trees where we could hide for the day."

"We saw your chief come," Melemele said. "But why does your chief want you to send us to him?"

"It's not you," 'Imi said. "It's only the fruit."

"To get the fruit, you must cut down the tree," Polapola said. "And that will kill us. We must go."

"No, don't," 'Imi begged. "There is so much I can learn from you. I will find two other bunches of bananas and take them to 'Ānunu. But he will be angry, for he will know these will not be the fruit he saw. He will insist on coming back here with me, but he must not find you. You must hide."

Polapola and Melemele agreed. They were enjoying their visit in spite of the danger posed by 'Ānunu. But they would be safe for at least one more day. They moved further up into the valley and at dawn they took root at Wai-o-ke-oe, The-Spring-of-Murmuring-Waters.

The next day, 'Imi staggered down the valley to 'Ānunu's compound with two bunches of fruit. 'Ānunu looked at them in disgust. "How dare you bring me these scrawny bunches?" he demanded angrily.

"But they are the ones you picked out yesterday," 'Imi replied.

"They are not," 'Ānunu said.

"I'm sure these are the ones you pointed to," 'Imi said. "Perhaps you will come and show me which bunches of bananas you want."

'Ānunu called for his manele bearers and they set out for Manu-ahi. When they stopped at 'Imi's farm, 'Ānunu looked but, of course, the two large banana trees he'd seen were not there. 'Ānunu climbed down from his manele and went to look for himself. In the middle of the patch he came upon two large holes in the ground. "What are these?" he demanded.

"Two large holes in the ground," 'Imi replied.

"Yes," said 'Ānunu, "two large holes where two large banana trees grew just yesterday. Where did you put them?"

"No one can dig up a mature banana plant and put it anywhere," 'Imi protested. "To get the fruit, one plants the huli that grow around the trunk. If I'd cut down those trees, there would be a lot of rubbish about. Where's the trunk? The leaves?

I don't see them!"

'Ānunu stared hard at 'Imi. He didn't believe the farmer was telling the truth, yet everything he had said was true. One could not transplant mature banana trees. There was no rubbish. Maybe, just maybe, 'Ānunu thought, he'd mistaken where he'd seen those bananas. Climbing back into his manele, he ordered his bearers to continue up the valley.

Before long, 'Imi heard 'Ānunu call and ran to the small stream Wai-a-ke-oe where 'Ānunu stood looking into a banana patch. There, towering above the others, stood two banana trees, one tall and bold, the other shy and retiring. From their trunks and leaves hung two perfect bunches of fruit.

"There," said 'Ānunu. "Those are the two bunches I want. I'll send some men up tomorrow and you will cut those down and send them to me."

That night, 'Imi went to find the strange kupua in his banana patch. "'Ānunu came today," he said, "and I have done what I could but he will not be happy with the bunches I shall send him tomorrow. He'll come back again."

"We still have tonight to talk," Polapola said.

"We must leave here," Melemele said. "It is dangerous."

"Let us walk further up the valley," Polapola said.

The three of them walked further up Manu-ahi until they came to where the valley splits into two smaller valleys, Ka-pōhaku-kilo-manu and Ka-wai-puʻua. Where these two valleys join, 'Imi called Puhi because he had caught eels in the stream and here he had found a banana whose spotted skin reminded him of an eel. On the way, Polapola and Melemele told 'Imi about bananas: if planted on the night of Laʻau, the fruit will be heavy and the farmer will need to prop them up with poles so the tree will not fall to the ground; if planted on the night of Hua, the fruit will be small although there will be many bananas in the bunch. They told him that the best time of day to plant is at noon, for if the tree is planted when the shadows are long, the tree will grow long and spindly, and so noon is best when the shadows are directly overhead. Then the strength will go into the trunk and the fruit will mature more quickly than one planted in the morning. Polapola and Melemele told him how to wrap mature bananas in dried leaves and bury them in a pit or in a large gourd container, for such fruit is better flavored than those left to ripen on the plant. By the time they reached Puhi, it was very late in the night.

"Day is coming and we don't have time to reach our canoe," Melemele said, worried. "We must spend at least one more day."

"These maiʻa puhi are nowhere near as tall as we are," Polapola said. "We can't hide amongst them at all."

"If one of you will cut and carry tree branches here, and the other gathers pili grass," ʻImi said, "we can make a house to hide you."

"A great idea," said Polapola, grinning. "Of course we'll help."

As the sun rose, Polapola and Melemele stepped into the newly built house while ʻImi sat in the doorway sharpening his digging stick.

When ʻĀnunu's men came, ʻImi was waiting for them at Wai-o-ke-oe. "Now tell me which bunches to send down with you," he said.

The men looked and looked and finally chose two bunches that were the ripest and set off to take them to ʻĀnunu. ʻĀnunu was furious to be tricked again. He called for his manele and set out for Manu-ahi. This time he would not be fooled again. He would stay and have the fruit cut down before his own eyes and would carry them down in his manele.

ʻĀnunu climbed out of his manele and stood over ʻImi as he sat in the doorway of his house at Puhi.

"What kind of a fool do you think I am?" ʻĀnunu demanded. "How dare you send such spindly dried up tasteless fruit? Where are the bananas I saw and you saw? Where are they?"

ʻImi shrugged. "I only sent you what you ordered," he said.

"Nobody can be that stupid," ʻĀnunu said. "There are two large banana trees somewhere in Manu-ahi. Each tree has a huge bunch of ripe fruit. The fruit smelled wonderful, and I smell them right now."

ʻĀnunu sent three of his carriers to search Ka-pōhaku-kilo-manu and the other three to search Ka-wai-puʻua. Before the men finished their search, night was falling. "I'll spend the night here," ʻĀnunu announced. "Tomorrow I shall search Manu-ahi from one end to the other. I will find those trees and I will take the fruit."

The six carriers returned. "We have not found those trees," one of them said. "We have searched everywhere except in 'Imi's house." The men laughed at the joke.

"Do you think I'd plant bananas inside a house?" 'Imi laughed, too.

"I will use your house to rest in," 'Ānunu said, "while you prepare me a meal. Get out of the way," he said to 'Imi who was sitting in the doorway.

As 'Imi sat there, his heart breaking, two people appeared in the doorway behind him. It was night and Polapola and Melemele had regained their human form. Frightened, 'Ānunu's men threw themselves on the ground and buried their heads in their elbows. 'Ānunu's jaw dropped and he stared with eyes bigger than any owl.

Polapola said to 'Imi, "Thank you for your hospitality and for your friendship. It would have been easy to simply cut down the banana tree and send your chief the fruit."

Melemele said, "You, 'Ānunu, have proved you are greedy. These bananas were the first to be seen on Kaua'i, yet you would have cut them down before the young huli began to grow. You wished to feast on the fruit with no thought for the future."

"Now hear us," Polapola said. "'Imi, inside this house there are huli, young shoots which you know how to plant and care for. Take them and plant them in all the new places you discover on this island. Then there will always be food to eat on Kaua'i when other islands suffer famine."

"And you, 'Ānunu," Melemele said, "because of your greed, no longer will you be able to taste any food. However, if you help 'Imi, if you make sure that these bananas may be eaten by both men and women and that your high chief will not tabu them for his own use, if you become a guardian of your people, helping rather than taking from them, then little by little you will regain your sense of taste."

Polapola and Melemele went back to their canoe and sailed away to their home in the heavens. Each night they looked down on Manu-ahi. They watched 'Imi continuing his search for new bananas, and watched him care for the mai'a hilahila, the shy banana, and the mai'a lele, the leaping banana. They watched as 'Ānunu really tried to change and became careful to preserve his people's food, sending the best to his great chief Kū-alu-nui-kini-akua, but keeping only for himself nothing better than that which his poorest farmers ate. Slowly, slowly, 'Ānunu's food came to taste good again to him.

'Imi passed on to his sons all he had learned from Polapola and Melemele. He showed these young farmers how to plant bananas so they would grow well. He taught them the secrets of each kind and sort of banana. When his long life was over, Polapola and Melemele came for him and took him in their canoe and brought him to their home. Now the three of them look down at Kaua'i from Ka-honu-moku, three stars in a row in the northern skies known as the Mai'a-kū, which we know as the Belt of Orion.

KE KŌLOA O KAIKAPŪ

CHRISTINE FAYE 88

aikapū guarded the Koloa shoreline, keeping everyone away from the swimming places and from the food on the reefs and in the sea. She was a moʻo, one of the great lizards of Kauaʻi of long ago. She swam up and down the coast, keeping a close guard for a careless human to wade onto the reef or attempt to catch a fish. Her favorite trick was to hide herself in the rocks around the point where the Waikomo stream enters the ocean, listening for sounds of people. She would then swim furiously around the point and grab a fisherman from the rocks or a swimmer near the shore as she swept by.

Soon no one living in Koloa dared to come to the ocean. No one had fish to eat. No one gathered the golden brown līpoa seaweed used to flavor their food. No one could work at the natural rock pans where ocean water evaporated leaving salt crystals. People could only gather on the high ground and stare longingly at the sparkling ocean where Kaikapū swam and waited patiently for her next meal.

Liko and his grandmother also stared in hopeless anger at the huge moʻo playing in the surf beyond the reef. They lived on the hill above Kukui-ʻula bay, and below them a leaf of rock spread into the ocean. Here waves crashed against the rocks and the water bubbled up from a large hole in the center of the leaf. However, no one dared to go to pick ʻōpihi from the rocks near the hole because Kaikapū would sweep past, stretching her long neck to snatch the fisherman in her jaws. Liko's grandmother sighed. "I would like a taste of iʻa hoʻomelu," she said. "I dream of the delicious pieces of raw hīnālea fish mixed with red salt, roasted kukui nuts and brown līpoa seaweed." Even though some people thought this fermented relish had an offensive smell, Liko's grandmother loved to spice her poi with it.

Liko had been raised by his grandmother. She taught him from the time he could talk to memorize the genealogy of their family, the names of family members, from the ancients now gone to all the living aunts, uncles, nieces, nephews, and cousins. She taught him the family prayers and the historical legends in which family members had played a part. He was to become the head of the family once she was gone. It was a position of great responsibility and of great honor.

So when she sighed, "I would like a taste of i'a ho'omelu," Liko decided at once she would have it.

He stared at Kaikapū. The mo'o was as large as the whales that sometimes played offshore and just as fast. No one could outswim her. Even a canoe under sail could not move through the waves faster than she. He stared down onto the rock leaf, remembering the days before the mo'o when he and his friends would play there where the water boiled up from a tube that opened into the sea. Once when the tide was very low and the waves very flat, they had peered through the tunnel and could see the sunlit water at the other end. He looked along the coast remembering the places where he had gathered līpoa and the holes where the shy hīnālea fish lived.

Kaikapū swam to the edge of the rocky leaf and stared hungrily at the young man standing on the bluff. She, too, was hungry for her favorite food. She dove beneath the water and hid herself. Perhaps, just perhaps, the young man would dare to come down to the water's edge and then, then! Kaikapū would eat again.

Liko watched Kaikapū dive. She did not come up again. She was hiding, he knew. He put a finger to his eyelid and pulled it down, a gesture at once an insult and a show of defiance.

"Lizard or no lizard," he muttered, "I'm going to catch a hīnālea and gather some līpoa."

Below him a wave surged up through the hole in the rocks. The water poured back into the hole and Liko smiled. He had an idea.

He ran home and got his short spear made of heavy kauila wood, sharp at both ends and very strong. He picked up his funnel-mouthed hīnālea trap woven from 'inalua vine. He returned to the edge of the rocks, grasped his spear and fish trap and dove into the water, kicking hard to reach some rocks where he anchored the fish trap. His lungs grew tight, hurting from the lack of air, and he surfaced.

As he tread water, Liko heard a loud snort behind him. Twisting around, he looked up into the evil face of Kaikapū. Smiling a lizard's smile, Kaikapū opened her jaws to grab Liko. The young man pounded the water with cupped hands and yelled loudly as though chasing a shark away. The mo'o, surprised at this show of defiance, paused just a moment and Liko swam towards the rocks as fast as his arms could take him.

Liko heard the moʻo churn the water behind him and he dove to hide among the rocks. He heard the dull click of the lizard's mouth closing behind him as she missed her prey. He hooked his feet behind a rock and turned to face his enemy, holding his sharp spear in both hands.

Kaikapū grinned and swam slowly up to Liko. She knew she caused anyone this near her to become so afraid he could offer no defense. She opened her jaws wide and moved in for the kill.

Liko turned his spear so one end pointed to her upper jaw and the other pointed to her tongue. Kaikapū's jaws snapped shut as Liko snatched his arms out of danger. Her jaws shut but instead of warm man-flesh, Kaikapū felt sharp pain as the spear drove through the soft tissue of her mouth. Kaikapū screamed with pain, tossing her head to shake off the spear.

Liko surfaced to catch his breath. He saw his grandmother standing at the water's edge, her arms stretched high above her head.

"Kaikapū!" she called, "Here I am. Take me instead!"

"No!" Liko yelled. "Grandmother, go back!"

Kaikapū hissed with rage. She saw the figure on the rocks but the one who had hurt her was still in the water. Her only thought was to punish him as she hurled herself through the water.

Liko dove down and searched for the opening of the lava tube that led to the rocky platform above. He saw it after agonizing moments and swam swiftly into it. He prayed to all his family gods to protect him. He did not permit himself to think what would happen if the tube was too small for him to go through. Better to die here, he thought, than end as a meal for Kaikapū.

Kaikapū saw the flutter of his feet as he slipped into the hole and with a bellow of rage she charged after him. She never considered her own size and the size of the tunnel. She was in pain and he who had caused this pain was just there. She sped into the hole behind Liko as a large wave surged against the rocks and a column of water poured in behind man and moʻo.

Liko struggled up the narrowing tube, his lungs hurting in the need for air. Fear lent him strength and he pushed against the sides, propelling himself forward. He did not feel the sharp rock edges cutting him. The surge of the wave caught him and threw him high into the air. He landed on the rocks beside the water hole. He was safe! He fell to his knees and offered a prayer of thanks to his family gods.

His grandmother rushed to him and with trembling fingers reassured herself he was alive and that his cuts were shallow and would soon stop bleeding on their own. "I thought you were dead!" she cried. "No amount of hīnālea or līpoa is worth your life. I must learn to be careful what I say."

Just then another wave surged against the rocks. Liko and his grandmother heard a dull roar coming from the lava tunnel. He struggled from his grandmother's embrace and ran to the opening.

"Listen, grandmother!" he said.

Suddenly a geyser of water blew out of the hole, a column of water twice as tall as the young man. This column of water spouted from the hole again as once more they heard the dull prolonged roar echoing from the lava tube.

"It's Kaikapū!" Liko cried. "She's caught in the lava tube!"

And it was as he said. Kaikapū had swum so fast into the tube that she wedged herself forever there.

From then on, the seashore was free for everyone's use. Liko could catch all the hīnālea his grandmother could eat. He caught hīnālea and gathered golden-brown līpoa seaweed often, for he liked to go down to the blowhole where Kaikapū lay trapped.

Even today when the column of water shoots high into the sky, an angry roar echoes from the tube, ke kōloa o Kaikapū. Kaikapū is still caught there and roars, angry and hungry, whenever the water rushes past her.

PALILA

he day Palila was born lightning flashed, thunder roared, and rainbows arched above his birthplace at Ka-mo'o-loa. White-haired Hina, priestess of the temple of Humu'ula, looked down the long ridge and smiled, very pleased with the success of her plans. Her daughter, Mahi-nui, had tarried too long in Koloa and her child had been born far from the sacred birthstone of Wailua-nui-hoana. Palila would not be a ruling chief of Kaua'i since he had not been born in Sacred Wailua but, Hina knew, for it was part of her plan, that would not prevent him from becoming a ruler somewhere else.

Hina descended the long ridge of Ka-mo'o-loa and came to where her daughter Mahi-nui and her husband Ka-lua-o-pālena were gazing at their new born son.

"I have come for the child," Hina said. "I will raise him."

It was the custom in the old days for a couple to give a child into the care of one of his grandparents and Mahi-nui and Ka-lua-o-pālena were pleased. Hina was a powerful priestess while they were young and would have more children.

"Where is the child's afterbirth?" Hina demanded.

Mahi-nui shrugged. "I don't know," she said. "It must have been tossed out in the rubbish."

"Foolish child! Stupid woman!" Hina scolded and rushed to the rubbish pit. There lying on top was the afterbirth looking like a piece of cord. It was intact, Hina noted with relief. No rat had chewed it, no bird pecked it. Hina picked it up and wrapped it in a piece of white tapa and returned to Humu'ula with the child in her arms.

She built a cradle of uluhe fern and placed the baby in it. "Your name shall be Palila," she said to the infant, "Palila, the yellow honeycreeper of the forests of Mauna-kea. For it is on Hawai'i you shall rule, Palila!" Hina had been born and raised in Hilo and her sister still lived there and it was for this birth she had come to Kaua'i.

Hina laid the tapa-covered bundle containing the afterbirth on the altar of her temple and prayed as she offered sacrifices to the gods. Then she unwrapped the bundle and placed the cord in a clean piece of white tapa. This she did two more times as the days passed. On the tenth day, when she unwrapped the bundle, the afterbirth was gone.

Hina exulted. The gods had agreed to her plans.

Palila grew rapidly and as soon as he had reached the age when he could take solid food, he was given nothing but bananas for nourishment. A special banana patch was created for him at Wai-oloio along the banks of Wailua river. The gods blessed the grove and the fruit and Palila thrived on these sacred bananas.

When Palila was old enough to leave the women's eating house and put on a malo, Hina took him further up the mountain to the heiau of 'Ālana-pō. This temple was very old and no one could remember when it had been built. It had been sacred to the gods from the beginning of time, whence its name, Freewill-offering-of-the-night. The priests of this temple offered strong prayers asking those who were on their way to Pō, the land of the dead, to give of the knowledge they had gained in this life. Those who were raised here were noted for their skills and strength and bravery. Here Hina brought Palila.

At 'Ālana-pō, Palila developed great skill and strength. He learned to box and wrestle, to catch a spear from the air and use it to fend off other spears flying at him. Even twenty men throwing their spears could not harm him. But his favorite weapon was the war club. The priests taught him how to shape his own club from kauila wood so that its balance was perfect. As he grew he made new war clubs to match his changing size and strength.

One day Palila said to his grandmother, "Now I know enough. I hear the sounds of war down below at Koloa and I wish to fight."

Hina turned to his teacher Hulu-mānienie. "Is he fully trained?" she asked.

"You shall see for yourself," Hulu-mānienie replied. They watched as Palila caught twenty spears thrown at once. They watched as he boxed, wrestled, and fought with the war club. When at last Palila stood before Hina and Hulu-mānienie, Hina said, "Indeed, you have learned well but you have learned only half of what there is to know."

"Only half?" Palila said, surprised.

"Everything you do," Hulu-mānienie explained, "you do with your right hand only."

"But everyone fights right handed!" Palila protested.

"Not everyone," Hina said. "Some are left handed. Your training is not complete. When you can use all your weapons with your left hand as well as you do with your right hand, then you will be free to join the war below."

The day came very quickly when Hina watched Palila defeat all his opponents. He could wield his weapons from hand to hand with such speed and dexterity that his bewildered opponent could not defend himself, having no idea from which direction the blow that would fell him was coming. Hina was pleased. She led Palila into the temple. Here she opened a gourd calabash. It took four men to remove a bundle of white tapa from the great gourd. Hina opened the bundle carefully, for the tapa was fragile with age. Inside the tapa was a war club made of polished red kauila, the strongest, heaviest wood known in Hawai'i. The club was large and long and down its sides gleamed rows of shining rows of shark's teeth.

"The name of this war club is Huli-a-mahi," she told Palila. "Huli means to hunt out and overthrow. Mahi means to dig the ground for planting. With this war club, you must seek out the wrong and prepare the ground for the right. Take it. It is a gift of the gods for you."

Palila, his eyes shining like the shark's teeth, grasped the war club. It fit his hand perfectly and although it had taken four men to lift it Palila easily swung it up over his head. He twirled it over his head, under his chin, around his waist and between his legs, switching from hand to hand with such speed that Hina laughed and said to Palila, "Now you are ready. Come down to the battle when you will."

Hina left Palila and went down to watch the latest battle. Kaua'i was at this time divided into two kingdoms. The west side, stretching from Mā-hā'ule-pu to Mānā was ruled by Na-maka-o-ka-lani. The east side stretching from Haupu mountain to Hanalei was ruled by Ka-lua-o-pālena. Na-maka-o-ka-lani wished to rule the entire island while Ka-lua-o-pālena was content to rule his lands in peace. Ka-lua-o-pālena however was a good strategist and had managed to keep Na-maka-o-ka-lani, in spite of his superior numbers of soldiers, from winning a decisive battle. Three battles had been fought so far and now the fourth battle was soon to begin.

If Na-maka-o-ka-lani won, the Kona chief would be the ruler of the entire island. The Kona chief had gathered all his soldiers, calling them from the hot sands of Mānā, from the deep valley of Mokihana, and from the rock-strewn plains of Wahi-awa.

Na-maka-o-ka-lani led his troops into Koloa and took up his positions. Some of the soldiers were camped in a deep wood that are guarded by the ridges of Lā‘aukahi on the west and Ka-lapa on the east that flowed down from the mountains like protective arms, flowing from the steep ridge that ran from Ka-mau-lele to Kō-ki‘i. The main part of the Kona army was drawn up on the plains of Weliweli facing the army of Ka-lua-o-pālena whose forces stretched along the borders of Pā‘ā from Ka-lae-o-ka-honu to Wai-o-pili spring. Here the two armies waited.

Early in the morning Hina came to Wai-o-pili where her son-in-law Ka-lua-o-pālena stood, studying the array of enemy forces before him. He wore his red and yellow cloak and feather helmet. A conch shell sounded from the Kona side and a messenger came forward and ran toward Ka-lua-o-pālena.

"My chief sends you greetings," the messenger said, "and says this. Look about you. Our forces outnumber you as the fish in the sea are more numerous than the breadfruit trees in the valleys. You cannot win this battle. If you will give up your lands, I will spare your life. If not, you will lose both lands and life this day."

Ka-lua-o-pālena replied, "I did not choose to fight this war. I am not greedy for land that is not mine. But now I will not call off any battle until I am victorious. I have lain awake many nights until my head was made heavy planning for this battle. Tell your chief I know that I will conquer the whole of Kaua‘i this day."

When the messenger had gone, Ka-lua-o-pālena turned to Hina. "Have I done well?" he asked.

Hina replied, "You must be on guard this day. Three warriors will come to offer their help to you. The first warrior who will come will be Ka-kohu-koko of Molowa‘a. Don't call him. The second will be Lupe-a-ka-wai of Wainiha. Don't call him either. But when a warrior comes twirling his war club in his left hand, that will be Palila your own son who comes from ‘Ālana-pō. He alone will be the warrior by whose aid you will conquer the whole island of Kaua‘i. Call him to you. If he is pleased with you, you will live. But if he gets angry with you, you will be slain together with your men."

Hina turned and went to a hilltop to observe the coming battle. She saw Ka-kohu-koko of Molowa‘a come across the plains of Pā‘ā with his war club. He was a short man, almost a dwarf, but he was very broad and heavily muscled. His strength was legendary. His war club was named Kawelo-wai, The Rippling-Water, because the warrior could twirl it with such speed that the surrounding air seemed to ripple like a pond's surface in a high wind. This club was so large that Ka-kohu-koko used eighty men to carry it from place to place, forty at one end and forty at the other.

This mighty warrior stood before Ka-lua-o-pālena and, taking up his war club, he swung it over his head a few times and then stood it on the ground, holding it with one hand to keep it from falling over. He flexed his muscles and made a series of fearsome faces to frighten everyone. All the Puna soldiers cheered loudly. With such a warrior on their side, how could they lose?

Chief Ka-lua-o-pālena however did not call Ka-kohu-koko to join him. The cheering died away until only the crashing of waves on the shore could be heard. Ka-kohu-koko became so ashamed that he returned immediately to his home in Molowaʻa.

Soon the Puna soldiers began to cheer again. Lupe-a-ka-wai of Wainiha had come. He was a very famous warrior, incredibly tall, almost a giant. It was said of him that every time he urinated the land was flooded. It was said he could defeat whole armies all by himself. He, too, came with his war club whose name was Kalalea, Prominent, for it was so large that Lupe-a-ka-wai used one hundred twenty men to carry it, forty in front, forty in back, twenty on the left and twenty more on the right.

When he arrived in the presence of Ka-lua-o-pālena, he picked up his war club and twirled it over his head and then down under his chin. The Puna soldiers cheered loudly, happy that such a warrior would be on their side. Lupe-a-ka-wai stood his war club on end and it was so heavy it sank down into the ground a little way. Lupe-a-ka-wai made faces sure to strike terror into the enemy and strutted about his war club waiting for the high chief's invitation to join him.

Ka-lua-o-pālena however remembered the words of Hina and did not invite Lupe-a-ka-wai to join his forces. When the warrior finally understood the chief did not want him, he was so ashamed he turned and went back to Wainiha.

But before the warrior that Ka-lua-o-pālena awaited could come, the Kona army of Na-maka-o-ka-lani attacked. Slowly the Puna army was pushed toward the mountains, toward the deep forest where more of Na-maka-o-ka-lani's army lay hidden.

The shouts and yells, the sounds of battle echoed across the plain and up the ridges into the mountains and woke Palila from his sleep. He rose to his feet, tied his malo tightly about his waist, took up his war club Huli-a-mahi and left the sacred temple of 'Ālana-pō. He came to a hill that looked down over the battlefield. Later this hill was named Komo-i-ke-anu, Coming-of-the-Cold, for many soldiers had seen a mighty warrior standing there and a chill fell across them as they wondered which side this warrior would join and so give the chill of death to the other side.

Palila looked down and studied the two armies. He saw the Puna army was smaller than the Kona army and was slowly being pushed back against the grove of trees tucked in the arms of Lā'au-kahi and Ka-lapa. The Puna army would surely lose, but it was a good battle and both sides fought fairly and Palila saw no reason to join either side. He was disappointed.

As he continued to study the battlefield, Palila came to realize the plan of Na-maka-o-ka-lani. The Kona chief had hidden soldiers in the woods and the unsuspecting Puna army would be attacked from the rear. Palila had been trained all his life to face his enemy squarely, to never turn his back, and to expect never to be attacked from the rear, for only cowards could shame their honor so beyond redeeming. Palila became angry.

He uttered his war cry which shattered rocks from the cliffs around him. The battle paused as everyone turned to look at the warrior standing on the peak above them. Palila swung Huli-a-mahi up and spun it and faster above his head and threw it. The club fled through the air, traveling at such speed that thunder followed it and the earth shook. Huli-a-mahi smashed into a tree at the edge of the woods. The tree fell onto another tree, knocking it down. So strong was the force of that first blow that trees kept falling one by one until all the trees had been knocked down. All of the Kona soldiers who had been hidden within the grove were destroyed. Palila chanted:

> You are slain by Palila,
> By the child of Hina of Humu'ula,
> By the warrior raised at 'Ālana-pō,

By the Palila singing in far-off mountains,
By the godly strength of Kū.

Thus, for the first time an enemy heard the death chant of Palila.

Na-maka-o-ka-lani withdrew his troops to their camp. The battle was over for the moment, but, the Kona chief vowed, it would begin again as soon as he could reorganize his forces.

Palila went down and stood before his father Ka-lua-o-pālena. The ruling chief of Puna looked at his son and saw a well proportioned youth, a man whose incredible strength could only have come from the war god Kū. Recognizing he was in the presence of godly power, Ka-lua-o-pālena fell to his knees and then stretched himself out face down on the ground.

Astonished, all of the Puna army fell flat on the ground, hardly daring to look up. As far as the eye could see only one man was standing, the warrior Palila.

Ka-lua-o-pālena said, "Child of the gods, hold out your club."

Palila stretched the club over the chief's head. "Where shall it go?" he asked. "Toward the uplands, towards the lowlands, to the west, or downward?"

The High Chief answered, "Where it can best feed on the pig and on the red fish."

Not even Hina, watching from her hill, knew what Palila would decide. Would he return to 'Alana-pō in the uplands, leaving the two armies to continue their fight? Would Palila decide to continue down and so come to the sea to take a canoe and sail away? Would Palila go to the west where the army of Na-maka-o-ka-lani was almost ready to attack again, and either defeat him or join him? Or would Palila smash the head of the chief lying in the dust at his feet? So many choices, Hina knew.

Even she was surprised when Palila placed the end of Huli-a-mahi on the ground before him and pushed the club deep into the ground until only the tip of the club showed. Then Palila pulled up his war club and water came welling up from the deep hole and trickled away among the fallen trees and dead soldiers.

Then Palila waited. He looked with surprise at all the men lying flat on their faces. Why don't they get up? he wondered. He looked at Hina for an answer, for she was walking through the living army toward him. "It is the kapu, the sacred kapu," Hina said. "Once a man prostrates himself before you, he may not rise, on pain of death, until you laugh."

"They will wait a long time, then," Palila said. "I have never laughed once in my life."

"So be it," Hina said. "We won't worry about that now. You are a warrior now who has tasted the blood of battle. Come." She led the way to the top of the hill 'Alea. Here with a sharp bamboo knife she slit his prepuce, a sign of a fully grown man, and tied around him a long malo of pure white tapa. This malo she named Īkuwā, Roaring-of-the-Forces-of-Nature. Then she placed a feather cloak about his shoulders and this cloak she named Haka-'ula, Red-shelf, for its feathers were red and Palila's broad shoulders were a shelf upon which would be placed the responsibility for the land Hina knew he would some day rule.

Then Hina undressed herself and, lying down on the ground, began to roll about on the backs of Ka-lua-o-pālena's army. This sight made Palila laugh for the first time and the kapu was broken. As the soldiers struggled to their feet, Hina dressed herself and went back to her home at Humu'ula. There was nothing more she could do for Palila.

With loud cries, the army of Na-maka-o-ka-lani swept toward the unprepared Puna men. Palila strode toward them alone, attacking them single handed. He used the high strokes and the low strokes of his club, changing from hand to hand, mowing down any soldier he met with a sweep of Huli-a-mahi. Ka-lua-o-pālena, inspired with new hope and courage, organized his troops and followed Palila into the battle. The two ruling chiefs met face to face and fought together. Ka-lua-o-pālena plunged his dagger through the rib cage of the Kona chief and Na-maka-o-ka-lani fell dead. The Kona army fled the battleground and at that moment, Ka-lua-o-pālena became the ruling chief of all Kaua'i.

After the battle, Palila removed the lower jawbone of each soldier he had killed and took them back to 'Ālana-pō to offer as sacrifices to the war god Kū.

The water continued to well up out of the hole Palila had dug with his war club Huli-a-mahi. This spring was named Wai-hohonu, The-Deep-Water. This water trickled away into the fallen trees and in time became a great lake of water which was named after the High Chief Ka-lua-o-pālena.

As for Palila he rested at ʻĀlana-pō for only ten days before he said farewell to his grandmother Hina of Humuʻula and left Kauaʻi forever. Hina had trained him well and she was proud of him. She watched him go with dry eyes and concealed the emptiness his leaving left in her heart.

KIA-KĀKĀ O PĀ'Ā

hief Ke-akia-niho picked up a morsel of octopus in his fingers, swirled it in his bowl of poi and popped it in his mouth. He hummed happily as he chewed. How he loved octopus! Now, because he had been a brave warrior, he had been rewarded as he felt he deserved.

Ka-lua-o-pālena, helped by his son Palila, had won the war against Na-maka-o-ka-lani and the island was at peace again. The winning high chief had rewarded his faithful followers and he had given Ke-akia-niho this ahupua'a of Pā'ā, land which stretched from the mountain peaks of Ka-mau-lele and Kō-ki'i to the ocean between Kāne-'aukai and Wai-o-pili. Since this also included all fishing rights, all the people who lived and worked the land growing gourds, sweet potatoes and taro, Ke-akia-niho was content.

He loved octopus to eat and Pā'ā was famous for the quantity and quality of its octopus. Even his physician and priest, the kahuna Kāne-a-ka-lua, had stopped grumbling because now there was a plentiful supply of octopus which he needed in his treatment of ailments.

Ke-akia-niho picked up the last bit of octopus from the bowl. He handed the calabash to his steward. "Fill it," he ordered.

The steward sped away and soon put in front of his chief a bowl of he'e-makole, octopus that had been cured with salt. "What's this?" the chief said. "I don't need to eat he'e-makole any more. There is a whole ocean full of octopus out there. I want fresh octopus."

The steward said, "There isn't any. The fishermen say that since the war has been over, the octopus have begun to disappear. There are fewer and fewer of them and they have gone very deep where it is hard to catch them."

"Very well, I'll go see for myself," Chief Ke-akia-niho said. "Send for my kahuna."

The steward sped off and in a short time the chief and his kahuna were on the reef peering into a pit known for good octopus fishing. Kāne-a-ka-lua unwrapped a lure made of a cowry shell.

Then holding out the lure in the palms of his hands, he prayed:

Oh, Kanaloa, god of the heʻe!
Here is the red cowry
To lure the heʻe to its death.
Here is the spear of kauila wood.
Here is the chief of Pāʻā.
Stir up the heʻe,
The heʻe of the deep blue sea,
The heʻe that inhabits the coral reef,
The heʻe that burrows in the sand,
The heʻe that spurts black water from its sac.
Oh, Kanaloa, god of the heʻe,
Stand upright on the solid floor,
Shake the floor where lies the heʻe,
Awaken the heʻe of the deep sea!
Let the heʻe take this lure!
God of the heʻe, Kanaloa,
Hear my prayer!

Kāne-a-ka-lua lowered the lure and danced it on the ocean bottom. Hour after hour passed and no octopus were caught.

"Kanaloa didn't hear your prayer," Ke-akia-niho said.

"He heard it. I could feel him helping me," Kāne-a-ka-lua replied. "There are just no octopus here."

"No octopus?" asked the chief. "Pāʻā is famous for its octopus."

"But no more," the kahuna replied.

"Why?" Chief Ke-akia-niho demanded, beginning to get angry. "There were a lot of octopus when we first came here. Now there are none. Perhaps your prayers are not good enough."

"Not even a god can catch octopus when there are none to be caught," the priest said. "There is something very strange about this. It is not natural. I must consult with the gods."

Kāne-a-ka-lua climbed the ridge of Ka-lua-hini until he came to the peak Ka-mau-lele. Here, after praying to the gods, he fell into a trance and released his living spirit, the 'uhane lele, into the air. The priest's spirit floated over Pā'ā, observing all that happened below. The afternoon passed and the sun went to rest behind the island of Ka'ula. The stars appeared, their light shone, and all the people from the chief to the fishermen fell asleep. Soon nothing moved in all the lands of Pā'ā. Only the coconut trees whispered and nodded to each other in the cool night breeze.

Still the priest's 'uhane lele kept watch. Finally, in the very darkest part of the night, a large 'alamuku crab crawled out of a hole near the sea. Kāne-a-ka-lua marveled. He had never seen so large a crab, almost as tall as a house, with claws that could easily grasp a man around the waist. Each of the eleven dark red spots on its back was as large as a poi calabash. No crab could ever grow so big without every fisherman in Pā'ā telling of it, so, the priest reasoned, it must be an 'aumakua, a family god and guardian. The prayer that could call up such a huge 'aumakua was indeed powerful.

In its claws, the crab carried fish netting and quickly scuttled over the rocks onto the reef and disappeared beneath the ocean.

The 'uhane lele of the priest Kāne-a-ka-lua asked the wind for this crab's name, but the wind didn't know for it came from the mountains and was only visiting the sea. The 'uhane lele asked a passing seagull but it didn't know either. He asked the coconut trees but they merely stared at him with their dark eyes and rustled their leaves. Kāne-a-ka-lua needed this crab's name for it is only by calling a thing by its proper name that one can control it. At last Kāne-a-ka-lua asked a small rat, the 'iole, "What is the name of the large crab?"

The rat replied, "Oh, his name is Kia-kākā."

The spirit of the kahuna pondered this name. A kia he remembered was a person who caught animals, like the kia manu who trapped birds for their brilliant feathers. Kākā was a way of fishing using square nets dropped in shallow water. Both bird catchers and fishermen were servants of chiefs. So, the kahuna reasoned, the name of this crab might indicate that it was the servant of a chief. There were other possible meanings, but the priest was content with this interpretation. The 'uhane lele of Kāne-a-ka-lua waited patiently for the crab to return.

Just before dawn, the crab returned with its nets filled with fish and from its claws dangled many octopus. There were some he'e-pū-loa, the long headed octopus, four mūhe'e that have only six tentacles instead of eight, and even a few he'e-māmoko which were seldom eaten because of their bitter taste. The crab clambered upon the rocks on its many legs and once on shore disappeared down a large hole in the ground. The 'uhane lele of the priest flew back to his body on Ka-mau-lele.

Even before the sun rose, the priest had returned to his chief and told him what he had seen and the chief had called together his soldiers and marched them down to the seashore. Knowing now what to look for, the hole in the ground was quickly found. Ke-akia-niho led the way into the hole, descending a staircase of rocks that had been raised from the bottom for that purpose. Inside there was a large cave that stretched back far beyond into the darkness. In the middle of the cave smouldered a small fire. Around the walls calabashes were dangling in their nets, heavy with the octopus and fish that the crab had brought in only a short time ago.

Kāne-a-ka-lua, just behind his chief, pointed to a man sitting beside the fire. Ke-akia-niho smiled grimly. The man his priest pointed to was the former chief of Pā'ā who had fought with Na-maka-o-kalani. Defeated, he and his men must have hidden themselves here.

Yelling his battle cry, Ke-akia-niho leaped upon his enemy and the two men fought hand to hand. Taken unaware, the enemy chief fought as best he could but he was no match for Ke-akia-niho whose anger was fed by the sight of the many octopus hanging along the walls of the cave. The enemy chief used his war club but it was too short against the long kauila wood spear of Ke-akia-niho. The enemy chief knocked away one end of the spear and was knocked on the head by the other as Ke-akia-niho twirled it with blinding speed from one side to the other. An arm broken, his head bleeding, the enemy chief threw aside his club and stood waiting for the final thrust of the kauila spear.

But Ke-akia-niho admired his bravery. He accepted the surrender of his enemy and allowed him to leave the lands of Pāʻā for an exile's life somewhere else.

The soldiers of Ke-akia-niho cheered their leader but Kāne-a-ka-lua raised his hand and, into the silence, said, "Take torches and come with me to search this cave for the crab. Be careful. It is as big as you are."

They searched the cave from one end to the other but they did not find the crab, Kia-kākā. In later days, the salt-sprayed rocks of Pāʻā were home to many ʻalamuku crabs, each bearing eleven red spots on its back. But these were small crabs and instead of catching octopus, they themselves were a meal for the heʻe that lurked in the pools of the reef.

The large crab was never seen again in Pāʻā. In time the octopus returned in great numbers. Whenever Ke-akia-niho sat down to eat, he always had a morsel of octopus to dip into his poi bowl.

KA PĀʻŪ ONAONA O HINA

have come," said Pele-'ula, "to see the beauties of Kaua'i for myself."

"I hope you will be pleased," replied Hina, pressing her nose to the nose of her visitor from Oahu.

It was a bright morning when no clouds obscured the mountains. Earlier, Hina, high chiefess of the island of Kaua'i, had been awakened by her steward Lā-anoano running in to announce breathlessly that a red-sailed canoe was even then entering Nā-wiliwili bay. Only high chiefs could use red sails and, being assured there was only one canoe and no one aboard seemed to be armed, Hina hurried down to the beach at Nuimalu to greet her visitor.

Pele-'ula was a chiefess of Waialua on Oahu. She was famous for her beauty and her court was noted for the loveliness of the women and the handsomeness of the men. Nowhere else was there such beauty, yet rumors persisted that the beauties of Kaua'i were even greater.

Kaua'i women were the most beautiful, it was whispered, Kaua'i men the strongest and tallest. Pele-'ula herself was lovely with lustrous hair, smooth skin, large eyes, graceful in movement, and yet...Pele-'ula decided to see for herself.

She greeted Queen Hina, smiling happily to herself. Here was no threat to Pele-'ula's reputation. Hina was taller than many men. Her hands were big, her feet broad. Her nose was a tiny bit too large, her figure perhaps a shade overripe, and her movements were forceful.

At Hina's order, her men leaped into the canoe, took the paddles from the tired Oahu crew, and rowed the two high chiefesses up the Hulē'ia river, past Alakoko fish pond, to where the Menehune's broken stone barred further progress upstream. Here the chiefesses were met and, side by side in a manele slung over the shoulders of men, were carried to the court of Hina nestled on the slopes below the mighty mountain peak, Hā'upu. There Pele-'ula rested the first evening.

Pele-'ula discouraged plans for a sight-seeing tour the next day. "I'm tired from my journey," she said. "I know the land of Kaua'i contains many beautiful places, but it's so tiring to visit them. I shall listen to your singers chant about them and I shall know the scenery as though I had seen it with my own eyes."

Hina chuckled. "If I cannot take you to the beauties of Kaua'i, I must do what I can to bring the beauties of Kaua'i to you. I think tomorrow night a little feast is in order, then a game of kilu."

"Good!" Pele-'ula said. "I shall look forward to it." She sank back on her pile of lauhala mats, enjoying the coolness of the Kipu air.

During the day, Hina's tapa makers beat out their secret code as runners sped to all the ahupua'a of the island. All chiefs and chiefesses were invited to Kipu to meet the famed beauty of Waialua. The next day chiefs wearing capes and feather helmets and chiefesses wearing lei palaoa around their throats and lei hulu in their hair crowded into the court of Hina.

Hina and Pele-'ula reclined on the same lauhala mats, equals and sisters in spirit, greeting each new arrival. During the morning, they greeted those who lived nearest the court and in the afternoon those who lived further away at Waimea and Hanalei. They came in twos and threes and fours, their attendants hovering about them waving feathered kahili, while large numbers of commoners brought food: live pigs dangling from poles, dogs trotting on their own feet, chickens cooped in calabashes, taro, sweet potatoes, limpets, squid, all brought as contributions to the feast.

The court was crowded and still dust rose along the distant roads announcing more guests. Pele-'ula eyed each woman carefully. There were many beauties among them, but no more so, she thought, than those she had gathered about her at Waialua. The men were tall and sturdy, but not, she felt, any more so than the Oahu chiefs she knew. A man's appearance was one thing but the manner and skill with which he used his weapons was more important. Pele-'ula tingled with anticipation for on the following day there were to be exhibitions of many skills: boxing, spear throwing, wrestling of all sorts, and mock battles. There would be much betting and Pele-'ula looked carefully at each man judging for herself which one might win over another and so be worth betting on. The day sped past and Pele-'ula thoroughly enjoyed herself.

Late in the afternoon a chief came. He was alone, no companion of his rank by his side, only a few attendants, and his elderly kahu holding the chief's kahili. Pele-'ula quickly sat up. Hina also sat up; their attention had been caught. This was a most handsome young man.

The chief came up to his hostess and her guest and greeted them and was taken away to find a place to stay. His name, he said, was Kahili and he had just become the konohiki chief of Kilauea ahupua'a.

Pele-'ula followed his departure with her eyes. "He's young," she commented.

"Not too young," Hina suggested. "He's had some experience."

"He's so tall," Pele-'ula said, "and wide shouldered."

"Long legged, lean hipped," Hina replied. "A lovely morsel for the one who can win him at kilu."

Pele-'ula laughed. "I am very skilled at tossing the kilu!"

"A score of ten wins the prize," Hina said.

"You and I against each other?" Pele-'ula asked. "Why not? We shall see which of us is the more skilled!"

Hina chuckled. "A game worth playing with a prize like that!"

The two chiefesses went down to a pond in the Huleia river to swim and bathe, then returned to be massaged and oiled, and dressed and adorned with lei, Pele-'ula with strands of yellow 'ilima flowers, Hina with a headpiece woven of laua'e fern fronds. The feast provided a sample of any food anyone could wish for, the red limu kohu from Molowa'a, red salt from Nomilu, 'ōhelo berries from Kapu-ka-'ōhelo in the far mountains; there was fish and pork, dog and chickens; taro leaves stewed in coconut milk, 'opīhī, pipipi, sea urchins and squid from the shore. There was laughter and chattering, teasing and banter. Pele-'ula, freed from the cares of being hostess, amused herself thoroughly. She kept her eye on Chief Kahili for he was pleasant to look upon. His skin was taut over his muscles. He would do well in the sporting events and, she decided, she would bet on him any time he entered a contest. She made no attempt to talk to him; plenty of time for that after the kilu game.

The feast was over. The presiding officer of the kilu game, Lā-anoano, called the players into a flower scented hall. The floor was covered with woven lauhala mats, piled so deep no cold could seep up from the ground to chill a player. Torches of kukui nut strings burned along the edges. Lā-anoano quickly tapped out ten players, Pele-'ula and Hina among them. To his surprise and happiness, Lā-anoano's wand touched the shoulder of Chief Kahili. Lā-anoano seated the five women on one side of the mat and the five men opposite them. A block of heavy wood, broad at the base and tapering to the top was placed before each player. Beside each block was set a kilu, an oval shallow cupped bowl made by cutting in two an egg-shaped coconut shell, highly polished and oiled. At a command from Lā-anoano, the ten players made a few test throws of their kilu. A kilu must be of such a balance and weight that, when thrown across the mat, it will not only slide but spin, giving some control of the kilu so that it will hit the block of one of the players opposite. A few kilu were exchanged, new ones tested, then the ten players began to look at one another and bantering began. Behind the players the guests crowded and speculated and laughed and made their own plans for later.

Lā-anoano raised his wand and everyone fell silent. He chanted a prayer to the gods to free all those under the roof from any kapu and then said, "Let the first throw go to our guest from Waialua."

Pele-'ula smiled at the gesture of hospitality and, turning to Hina, suggested, "We claim the same prize. Let's take turns. Ten strikes wins the game."

"Done," said Hina. She summoned Lā-anoano and explained to him.

"This is a different game," he protested. "What of the others?"

The crowd buzzed with curiosity.

Lā-anoano crossed the mat and knelt beside the young chief. "You have made a conquest, or rather two, the beautiful chiefess from Oahu and our own Queen Hina. They wish to play against one another with you as the forfeit. Are you willing?"

Kahili looked across the gaming mat at the two women who avoided his glance by chatting together. How could he not be flattered? His pride swelled and he nodded. "I'm willing," he said.

After a brief whisper to Hina and Pele-'ula, Lā-anoano quieted the crowd to announce the change in the game. The remaining players cheerfully hung their kilu on top of their markers. The crowd yelled its approval.

"Let Kahili tell of himself!" shouted one on-looker and the cry was taken up around the hall. Usually a boast was chanted by a player before throwing the kilu, but this was new, even before the game was begun a choice was made. Kahili would not have to throw a kilu and already he had won! Let the cock strut before his hens!

Kahili stood. His only adornment was a lei palaoa and his malo. The lamplight shone on his skin, he sang, his voice deep and rumbling. A drummer picked up his rhythm. The chief began to dance, a dance that moved the muscles of his body like a school of fish moving through the ocean.

> Wreath of yellow flowers from Waialua,
> Wreath of laua'e fern from Limahuli,
> Glorious flowers!
> Here are the bones of Ko'olau,
> The 'ulu, breadfruit tree and warrior, of Kilauea.
> Let us play a game of pahe'e with darts of sugar cane tassels,
> And weave ourselves lei of puhala fruit.
> Let us spread an 'ahu hinano, a mat of the pandanus flowers,
> And dance through the night
> Turning at dawn, drenched with dew, to our companion.
> Come ride the flood of Hanalei!
> Glorious flowers!
> Together we two!

As Kahili sat down again behind his marker, the crowd shouted their approval. Glorious flowers! What warrior could ask for more?

Lā-anoano once again quieted the spectators. "Let the first kilu be thrown!" he ordered.

Pele-'ula said, "This kilu is a love token, the forfeit a kiss!" With a twist she sent her kilu spinning across the mat. It struck the marker in front of the handsome young chief. The crowd applauded and happy teasings accompanied Pele-'ula as she crossed the mat to bestow her prize, Pele-'ula's kiss.

Now it was Hina's turn. "This kilu, too, is a love token, its forfeit a kiss." She flung the kilu across the mat and it struck Kahili's marker with a ringing noise. Once again the crowd erupted in applause and teased their chiefess as she crossed the mat.

"I think the young man will win many kisses tonight," Lā-anoano remarked. "These women are skilled kilu throwers."

Indeed he was right. Pele-'ula threw her kilu and it always struck home. Nor did Hina miss her target. Then each had thrown their kilu nine times and Kahili had received eighteen kisses. He was burning, he was cold, his legs trembled, his body ached with anticipation. Which one? The crowd roared and laughed and made extravagant bets. Hina would win! No, Pele-'ula would win!

Lā-anoano raised his baton and silence fell over the crowd. No one moved as Pele-'ula rose to her feet and she sang.

> My lover dances like the parrot fish of Makapu'u,
> His face shines like the lighthouse of Lae-o-ka-la'au!
> No upright cliff is womanless in this place!
> Vigorous grows the cliffs of Ulamao!
> You belong to me!

Deftly she tossed her kilu. The polished coconut shell spun across the mat and struck home! The crowd roared, screaming with joy, pounding one another's backs, tossing flowers toward the high chiefess of Waialua. Kahili leaped to his feet to claim his kiss.

Yet the game was not over. Lā-anoano once again raised his baton and again the crowd stilled. Hina rose and, like her guest, sang.

> My friend is blown to me by the tapa tearing winds of Kalalau,
> Blown from the towering cliffs of Makua-iki,
> From the hanging ladder of Nualolo, he is blown to me.
> You belong to me!

She tossed her kilu and, as surely as the honeycreeper is drawn to the lehua blossom, the kilu flew across the mat and struck Kahili's marker.

"Ten!" cried Lā-anoano. "Ten for Pele-'ula, ten for Hina!"

The crowd waited, open-mouthed, eyes as wide and shining as the mother of pearl eyes of the god of birds, Kū-huluhulu-manu. No one moved an arm or a leg but their eyes darted from face to face. What would happen? The two women had battled for the chief of Kilauea, both had won him. How would they settle this?

Hina turned to Pele-'ula. "You were the first to have ten points. He is yours."

"No," replied Pele-'ula, "we have both struck his marker fairly."

Lā-anoano said, for as gamemaster he had been wondering what to do if such an occasion arose, "Since the gods have directed your kilu with equal skill, it seems the gods cannot decide whether Kaua'i or Oahu holds the most beauty. Therefore let the chief choose. Let each Chiefess clothe herself, and adorn herself to be at her best. Each will compose a song for the occasion and will dance it."

The two chiefly women nodded their agreement. Hina said, "See that Pele-'ula has everything she needs, Lā-anoano. Never shall it be said that Kaua'i is stingy with hospitality. And as for Chief Kahili, he is kapu. Let no one touch him. He is the prize for one of us. When shall we meet again?"

"Five nights from now," Pele-'ula answered.

"Agreed," Hina said. "Lā-anoano, see to it."

On the fifth night, after days of sport contests when Chief Kahili won his share of championships, eager spectators crowded the dance shed. Behind tapa curtains stretched across opposite corners to form alcoves, Pele-'ula and Hina made their last preparations as Lā-anoano led Chief Kahili to his seat. A large lauhala mat served as a dancing platform. At one end of the mat a row of musicians nervously tapped their gourd drums or blew a tentative note into bamboo flutes.

Lā-anoano strode into the center of the hall and, lifting his baton, waited for silence.

"Chief Kahili, the choice is yours. Our guest shall be first."

A musician raised his flute and began a melody as another began to twirl his 'ūlili, a set of three gourds pierced by a stick, in a sharp beat. Pele-'ula stepped onto the mat, already in motion, one heel raised at a time keeping time to the beat. She wore a pāʻū hanina, a dress stained yellow in its making by ʻōlena roots. A lei of brilliant yellow feathers was wound in her hair and she wore long strands of ʻilima flowers native to her Oahu homeland. The crowd murmured its appreciation as it recognized the hula ʻūlili, the dance of the wandering tattler, the shore bird that dances with the edges of ocean waves. As she danced, Pele-ʻula chanted.

> My search for a sweetheart
> Is a pleasant diversion on this night,
> A night at the foot of Hāʻupu.
> Every two days the Wai-opua wind shifts its source,
> Now rustling in the uplands,
> Now blowing to the heights of Wai-aloha.
> The laughter of rain in the forest
> Gathers affection there
> Like birds sipping nectar from the lehua tree,
> And brings it to this multitude below.
> All this work for a sweetheart!
> So join with me, let us be together,
> Let us enjoy the winds of Koʻolau-wahine!
> Caught, caught,
> Caught is my bird
> By the sight of ʻilima from Waialua!

The dance was over. Pele-ʻula went and sat beside the young chief, leaning against his knee. She was flushed by her dance, sure of victory, yet curious to see what her rival would do.

Hina stepped to the center of the mat and stood in regal silence until all whispering had stopped and every eye was upon her. Her pāʻū was very thin, a gauze only the most skilled tapa maker could produce and only on Kauaʻi was it made. The outer layer of her skirt was dyed green and the four underlayers were of palest green. The feather lei perched like a crown on her head was made of green feathers from the 'amakihi, the birds that lived no where else but in the forests behind Wai'ale'ale. Her neck was garlanded with strands of maile, honoring the five Maile sisters born on this island, and of mokihana berries, plants unique to Kaua'i.

Hina gestured to her musicians and as she moved with the notes of the bamboo flute and the beat of the gourd drum, the scent of laua'e fern and mokihana berries, which had been pounded into the tapa of her pā'ū, filled the dance shed. As she danced, she told the story of the famous Kaua'i lovers of time past and it seemed to those who watched her that all the beauties of Kaua'i, its land, its history, its special skills found no where else, were gathered together here in this hall, in this one person, Hina, ali'i wahine o Kaua'i, Hina, the queen of Kaua'i.

> Climb up into the forest of Aipo,
> Come greet Ka-wai-kini,
> Look down to Pihana-ka-lani
> Where clothed in feathers,
> Seated next to his sister Ka-hale-lehua,
> Rests the lover, Ka-ua-kahi-ali'i.
> Come, Ka-ili! Come, Ka-ili!
> Come, Ka-ili-lau-o-ke-koa!
> Seek your husband in the uplands!
> The flowers of Lehua-wehe
> Lead to the waterfall of Wai-ehu
> That cascades and catches the heart
> And promises love amidst the ferns of Ke-wa!
> Surf on the waves of Maka-iwa!
> You are as shy as the maiden-hair fern
> at Wailua-nui-hoana.
> My house awaits, no attendants here.

For here are the sweethearts of forest and sea,
Ka-ili-lau-o-ke-koa!
Ka-ua-kahi-aliʻi!

Pele-ʻula sensed the moment when the young chief forgot her, when the evocation of the incomparable scenery of Kauaʻi cast its spell; when the comparison of the dancer and the chief to the famous lovers took the young chief far from the memory of Pele-ʻula, the beauty of Waialua. The perfume of the fragrant pāʻū of Hina, ka pāʻū onaona o Hina, had overpowered all challenge.

"I have now seen," Pele-ʻula thought, "the beauties of Kauaʻi for myself!"

The sound of flute and song died away. Hina stood, caught in the emotion of her song. Chief Kahili rose and went to her. The two looked at each other for a moment and kissed.

The crowd roared. Pele-ʻula, graceful in defeat, hugged Hina.

"You must give warning to those who, like me, think they can best the beauties of Kauaʻi!"

Hina said, "Lā-anoano, see to it."

Lā-anoano gathered skilled workers and on the ridge below Hāʻupu mountain they carved a likeness of Hina, her finger lifted in warning.

"Be warned," she seems to be saying, "the beauties of Kauaʻi are beyond compare!"

KA ULA MAI'A A PALILA

hen Nā-maka-o-ka-lani, high chief of Waimea, saw Palila striding down the ridge with his war club over his shoulder, he was filled with dread.

"Who is that?" asked Kulaina who stood behind the chief's left shoulder, her sling held in her right hand, her left resting on the pouch of water-polished stones.

"A kupua, a man with supernatural powers," her brother Ka-ma'a-lau guessed. He stood behind the chief's right shoulder. Brother and sister were inseparable and because they were both brave and fearless and were adept with all weapons, they had become the protectors of their high chief's back. Wherever Nā-maka-o-ka-lani went, there, too, like shadows, were Kulaina and Ka-ma'a-lau.

The three watched Palila. He was very tall, very broad across the shoulders, and carried his huge war club with insolent ease. Ka-ma'a-lau wondered if he and his sister together could even lift that club. Palila's skin shone with the oil that had been spread on it and his hair was long and free. He wore no insignia or rank, no helmet or cape, and his malo, with its flaps front and back, showed him to be an untried warrior, new to the battlefield.

"Yes, he's a kupua," Nā-maka-o-ka-lani said. "He was raised by his grandmother, the kahuna Hina. He will defeat us. Our men will be afraid to face him on the battlefield."

"Let me challenge him to a single battle," Ka-ma'a-lau asked.

"No," the chief replied. "He has supernatural powers. There is only one chance. I have heard that he gets his strength from eating bananas from a special grove on the banks of the Wailua river. Destroy the banana grove and his strength will fade. If he doesn't have enough strength to lift his war club, he can be defeated."

The chief looked at Palila, now standing on a knoll studying the battlefield below, leaning on his club of polished kauila wood. Nā-maka-o-ka-lani turned to his body-guards. "We can continue for three days against Palila," he said. "But no more bananas must reach him."

Brother and sister left their chief and sped on their journey to Wailua. By late afternoon they reached the edge of Mauna-kapu and were peering down into the river valley. To their east a broad expanse of water flowed to the sea and a little way to the west the river split into two branches. Below them was a grassy flat land with a grove of silver-green kukui trees and edging the deep pond named Wai-oloio was the grove of bananas dedicated and sacred to Palila. Across the river rose Kua-moʻo, Lizard's backbone, the undulating ridge followed by the path into the sacred land of Wailua-honua-nui. At the peak of the ridge on the edge of a steep cliff that fell five hundred feet into the river sat Poli-ahu heiau. From their lookout, brother and sister could see the walls of black rock and wooden heads of grimacing gods peering over them and the oracle tower covered with gleaming bleached tapa, untattered as yet by the trade winds, signifying newly accomplished ceremonies preparatory to the war now being fought at Koloa. Hulu-mānienie was the high priest there, second in knowledge and power only to Hina, grandmother of Palila and the kahuna nui of ʻĀlana-pō.

Across the river a conch shell trumpet sounded and a small double canoe left the shore. On the platform between the hulls stood a man, the ends of his white cloak, knotted at one shoulder, fluttered in the air as the paddlers drove the canoe swiftly upstream. Beside him, holding the pūloʻuloʻu sticks of spiritual power, two men stood. In front sat a drummer, beating out a warning that the high priest was about his official business. The canoe touched shore and the three priests passed into the grove and disappeared into the dark green fronds. When they returned to the canoe, the two priests were carrying a ten-hand bunch of ripening bananas. The three climbed aboard and the canoe crossed the brown river to its starting place. The bananas were given to two short muscular men and they started up the back of the lizard.

"Palila's bananas!" Kulaina said excitedly.

Brother and sister looked at each other. They had been born at the same time of the same mother and, through infancy and childhood they had not needed words to exchange thoughts, for indeed most of the time their thoughts were the same. So too this time. They had seen the runners start out and knew they had to cross the south fork of the river along the rocks above the swiftly flowing Wai-ehu waterfall.

"They must not reach Palila," Kulaina said.

As one they sped along the south fork and reached Wai-ehu falls before the two squat runners, their short muscular legs in step, the bunch of bananas swaying on the pole slung between their shoulders. They slowed to cross the river for the water was swift and the rocks slippery and a mis-step here would send them over the falls to drop a hundred feet to the rocks below. Kulaina placed a stone in her sling, twirled it over her head, each spin picking up speed, and let go. The man in front fell silently into the water and was swept over. The second man had only time to start in surprise when he too was felled by a stone from Kulaina's sling. Man and bananas swept over the falls.

Ka-maʻa-lau and Kulaina returned to Mauna-kapu where Ka-maʻa-lau rested until nightfall in the cave Anahulu while Kulaina stayed in Hauma, just below.

The moon was shining overhead as they planned the destruction of the banana grove. "We must get the ripest fruit first," Ka-maʻa-lau said.

For once Kulaina disagreed. "Let's start at this side and work toward the river," she said. "We must not be seen from the other shore until the grove is cut down."

Ka-maʻa-lau considered and shrugged his shoulders. "It doesn't matter how," he said, "just that the grove is destroyed. Let's begin."

They jumped down the slopes of Mauna-kapu and ran to the edge of the trees. With bamboo knives, they attacked the trees. Through the night they worked under the new moon until they were covered with slimey sap that made it difficult to hold their knives. There were only the two of them and there were countless trees and they were not trained farmers knowing what they were doing. As the first signs of dawn lit the eastern sky, Kulaina sighed in discouragement.

From the river came the drum beat of the high priest approaching the sacred banana grove of Palila.

"He knows yesterday's bananas did not reach Palila," whispered Ka-maʻa-lau. "We must hide and rest until he's gone."

Hand in hand they raced for the grove of flowering kukui trees, for they no longer had time to reach their caves. They hid themselves in a nest of fern under the silver-green kukui trees. They watched as Hulu-mānienie and his priests came into the banana grove and walked the path around the banana patch. The three came upon the fallen banana trees, the toppled trunks lying this way and that, unbroken leaves spread on the ground, the fruit trampled into the dirt. The two younger priests hurried into the devastation.

"Wind?" questioned one priest. "It can only be the wind."

"Pigs," said the other with conviction. "Only pigs can do this much damage."

They turned eagerly to hear Hulu-mānienie's decision, but the high priest looked at the fallen bananas, at the two priests, at the dusty path, at the steep slope leading to Mauna-kapu and said nothing. A faint smile hovered at his lips as he swiftly led his helpers into the patch, chose a bunch of bananas and sent the two priests staggering under its weight to the canoe. The drum sounded, paddles flashed, and the canoe skimmed downstream. Brother and sister, hiding in the perfume of kukui blossoms and crushed fern laughed with relief. After a time, they slept.

The moon rose early that evening and, as the sun sank to rest behind Wai-'ale'ale, it shone down into the valley of Wailua-honua-nui. There was no wind and only the gentle gurgle of the river as it flowed against the shore and the perfume of the kukui blossoms disturbed the quiet night.

Ka-ma'a-lau said, "Work quietly tonight. Hulu-mānienie must not hear us."

"Sounds are carried across the water and echo from the cliffs," Kulaina said. "But we have no choice. Palila must not defeat our chief." They both knew that, as the chief's guardians, they would become sacrificial victims to the gods of the winner and their bones, at the very least, would remain unburied.

"That is why we are here," Ka-ma'a-lau said and smiled at his sister. "Are you ready?"

"Where you go, I will follow," Kulaina said.

Ka-ma'a-lau and his sister came to the sacred banana grove of Palila, ka ulu mai'a a Palila, armed with axes of sharpened stone and knives of splintered bamboo. They stood, eyes searching for the bunches of fruit most nearly ripe, for they now realized it was better to destroy the trees with ripest fruit first, then work back to the freshest sprouts. Ka-ma'a-lau led the way into the grove to begin their night's work. He stood beside a trunk already beginning to fall, pulled toward earth by its heavy fruit. As he raised his axe, the air beside the trunk shimmered and the high priest of Poli-ahu, Hulu-mānienie appeared in front of the brother and sister warriors.

Ka-maʻa-lau dropped his axe, shame and humiliation filling him because he had, in spite of all his care and planning, been caught. For a warrior to be taken unaware, to be surprised so that the first blow could be struck by the opponent, was a humiliation so great, he could only bow his head and accept death proudly and with silent dignity.

Kulaina stifled a cry of dismay. She too was a warrior. She thought of her chief, of how they had tried to destroy the source of Palila's power, and was filled with a fierce joy that she would share her brother's fate. But she stared defiantly at Hulu-mānienie. She saw that she and her brother could easily overcome the priest physically, even though the man radiated a spiritual force that held her immobile. There was no way, she knew, she could rouse her brother to overcome his warrior's code, nor, she reflected, would she want that. They should have known the high priest would set a trap.

Hulu-mānienie spoke. "I have waited a long time for someone like you to come," he said. "Palila's grove needs a warrior to guard it from thieves."

"We are not thieves," Kulaina said angrily. "We haven't stolen anything."

"I know," the priest answered. "But others have stolen the fruit hoping to gain Palila's strength. Now your brother will stand guard and keep thieves and destroyers both away."

The priest gestured and began a prayer to the gods. Crying out in horror, Kulaina saw her brother turn to stone, larger than the man himself, taller than the trees so the guardian could look out over the entire banana grove to observe all the approaches to it. So tall had Ka-maʻa-lau become, he would warn all who came that there was a guard set over the grove and stood as an example of the fate a thief could expect.

Hulu-mānienie turned to return to the river. "You are free to go," he told Kulaina.

"No!" she cried. "I will not leave him!"

Silently the priest walked to the river's edge. A canoe, at his signal, sped across the water and he stepped into it. Kulaina ran after him, her knife raised to stab him. A paddler called a warning. The kahuna nui turned.

"Join him, then," he said, raising his arms in prayer. At the water's edge, Kulaina stumbled as she turned to stone and with a heavy splash fell into the waters of the river.

The banana grove of Palila is gone now and so is the power of the gods, overtaken by time and new religions. New plants have overrun the land. Still Ka-maʻa-lau on land and Kulaina under the water, twin brother and sister, stand guard until some day their duty will be over and they too will be gone.

KA MANUAHI

CHRSTINE FAYE 90

ina-a-ke-ahi sat in her eating house and lifted the lids of the calabashes made of coconut shells and of gourds. In one there was a dish of poki, a mixture of raw fish and limu līpoa. In another was a relish of hīnālea fish. In yet another was a mixture of mashed banana and water. Every morsel of food was as fresh as could be for the fish had been caught that morning by her nine sons and the bananas had been prepared by their hands. But all of it, she thought sourly, was raw, none of it was cooked.

She looked out the doorway of her eating house which stood on the cliffs above ʻŌpaekaʻa waterfall. Her eyes followed the stream to where it joined the Wailua river and followed that broad sheet of fresh water to the ocean. The sun shone brightly on the sea and sprays of white fume reminded her of the leaping flames she remembered before she had come to Kauaʻi, led here by a dream of a man, a man she had found here at Wailua-nui-honua, and married and bore his children.

Her nine sons were named Māui. The oldest was simply Māui, the youngest Māui-kiʻikiʻi. They were all tall, broad shouldered, legs as strong and shapely as the trunks of the ancient koa trees that grew on the mountains slopes. All had backs as straight as the pali down which flowed the waterfall of ʻŌpaekaʻa. But the oldest Māui was a natural leader. It was he who taught the others how to fish, how to plant, and how to get into mischief; he who was the most attentive to his mother. He had no secrets from her, but she held a secret of her own, one she could not tell him, one he would have to find out for himself. When, wondered Hina, would that time come?

She stared down at her food, drew in her breath and sighed so loudly that the breath ruffled Māui's hair as he sat outside her door.

"What's the matter, Hina?" he asked.

"Nothing," she muttered petulantly.

"Is something wrong with the food?" he demanded.

"No," she admitted. "But it's raw."

"Of course it's raw," Māui said. "What else could it be?"

"It could be cooked," Hina told him.

"Cooked?" he repeated. "What does that mean?"

"It means that the food is hot, that some plants like taro may be eaten if it is first steamed in an oven and then mashed like these bananas. It means to broil, to roast, to steam."

"And how does one do all that?" Māui asked.

"One finds fire," Hina replied.

It was on the tip of his tongue to ask, "What is fire?" but Māui thought he'd displayed too much ignorance already. His mother would become angry and his brothers would tease him and maybe no longer look up to him as their leader. Instead he only asked, "How will I know when I find fire?"

"You will see a thin plume of smoke, something like a cloud, coming from the fire; you will see red and yellow flames that will hurt your fingers if you try to hold them in your hands. You will feel the warmth of the sun at noon of a summer day at Mānā. Then you will know you have found fire."

"I shall keep a lookout for it," Māui promised.

"Good," said Hina and began eating her meal, still wishing it were warm and cooked.

Māui sat on the edge of the waterfall and looked down as his mother had done. He saw nine mudhens, the 'alae with black feathered bodies touched with white feathers under their tail and along their sides, their red bills tipped with yellow. They were swimming in the stream, their heads and necks moving back and forth as though it were this motion that caused them to glide along in the water instead of the action of their web feet beneath them. He saw the white breakers beyond the reef and caught sight of fish swimming there. Māui jumped to his feet.

"Brother!" he called. "I see a school of 'ahi out there. Down to the beach and into the canoe!"

The eight brothers ran down the ridge and by the time Māui arrived carrying his huge calabash that contained all his fishing lines and lures, the big canoe was ready. With a shout, the nine brothers pushed the canoe into the ocean and jumped in, paddles in motion, taking the canoe with a lunge past the breakers into the calmer waters outside. Māui stood at the prow of the canoe looking to where he had seen the school of fish but there was nothing there now.

"It's as though someone had told them we were coming," grumbled Māui the Eighth.

"Say, what's that?" said Māui-sixth, pointing to shore.

On the plain between ʻŌpaekaʻa and Alio beach there was a plume like a strange cloud climbing straight up into the sky.

"It's fire!" Māui shouted. "Paddle back to shore!"

As they paddled back, Māui-two asked, "Fire? Never heard of it."

"You will!" crowed Māui.

The brothers hurried ashore and ran for the place where they had seen the cloud plume but there was nothing to be seen on the plain. Māui looked carefully around him but there was nothing to see but a few piles of plant rubbish here and there, a pile of banana skins, a pile of fern fronds, broken branches of hau trees, nothing of any interest. There were the webbed footprints of the ʻalae birds but Māui had often seen them come ashore in this place and besides, what did the ʻalae know of fire? Māui was discouraged. There was no smoke, there was no fire, and there was no catch of ʻahi for dinner either.

From then on, whenever Māui and his brothers sailed out to sea after a school of fish they'd spotted from shore, the school of fish had disappeared and the strange plume of smoke climbed into the sky back on land. By the time they returned to shore, the smoke column was gone and there was no fire to be found.

One day, after spotting a school of big fish again, Māui said to his brothers, "You go out in the canoe. I shall stay here and hide in hopes I can see what happens here on land."

So with good cheer, Māui's eight brothers paddled out to sea. Māui hid himself in a small cave near the waterfall where he could look down into the valley of the column of smoke. But that day the brothers caught several of the large fish but there was no column of smoke.

This is what always happened. If Māui went with his brothers, the smoke appeared in ʻŌpaekaʻa valley and they caught no fish. If Māui stayed ashore, the eight brothers caught fish but there was no column of smoke. "That's good," Māui-three said. "If you stay ashore, we always catch big fish."

"Yes," Māui answered, "but Hina, our mother, must always eat it raw."

"You want fire, hiʻa, on the ground," teased Māui-three, "but you only have hiʻa, fire in the brain." Hiʻa, as a verb means to light a fire, while the noun hiʻa means the ability to think. It is the kind of play on words that delighted all Hawaiians.

"Hiʻa," Māui murmured. "Yes, I must think."

So he sat on his favorite rock on the brink of the waterfall and stared down at the nine ʻalae swimming up and down the stream, their necks and heads pumping like the forearms of a runner whose duty it is to deliver messages quickly from one place to another. And he thought. If he went out, smoke; if he stayed, no smoke. Therefore the problem was to be in two places at the same time, both in the canoe and on shore. And how was he going to be able to do that?

Just then Hina came out of her working house carrying a rolled-up bundle of tapa sheets she had finished making. It was heavy and she dropped one end and the roll buckled in the middle and for a moment, the tapa roll seemed to sit on the ground before toppling over. So life-like were its movements that Māui burst out laughing and then almost choked as the realization hit him. Here was the answer to his problem.

So, on the next fishing trip the eight Māui brothers paddled out to sea. On the last seat of the canoe sat a rolled up bundle of tapa that had been punched and buffeted and tied around the middle and neck to make it look as much like a man as it could. Māui himself was hidden in the little cave near the waterfall.

Shortly after the canoe had left shore, Māui saw one of the ʻalae mudhens fly to the top of the little hill called Mauna-kilo. The bird remained there for a bit, then flew down again, squawking loudly as it flew. It landed on the plain and was soon joined by its eight companions. They were too far away for Māui to see what they were doing, for there were nine birds and all of them were scurrying here and there on their ungainly feet but soon there was a little pillar of smoke climbing into the sky and all the birds were sitting around the base of it.

Māui rushed down as fast as he could but by the time he reached the plain, the smoke was gone and the birds had all flown far away. All there was were the footprints of the birds themselves, banana peels, and other plant rubbish. He stamped around and found a place where the dirt seemed warm, warm like the sands of Mānā on a summer's afternoon. Is this where the smoke had come from? Is this where the fire had been? Māui knew he had to hide himself closer so that the next time he could rush out and see for himself what these nine 'alae birds were doing.

That night, after the 'alae had swum away to their hidden nests to sleep out the night, Māui crept down onto the plain and dug a deep hole, big enough for him to hide in, and covered it over with sweet potato vines and banana leaves. Leaving orders with his brothers, Māui climbed into the hole, pulled the cover over him and waited.

At dawn, the eight Māui brothers, with the tapa roll riding in back, paddled out to the fishing grounds. One of the 'alae, the littlest one Māui noted, flew up to the hilltop and he could see it pump its head as it counted, one, two, three, four, five, six, seven, eight, and, yes, nine. Then the little 'alae flew back down and to Māui's surprise, for he did not know the 'alae could talk, said to the other birds, "There are nine in the canoe, so we know where the Māui brothers are and we will make a fire today."

The birds cheered and quickly began gathering plant rubbish and fresh bananas. These were all brought to the little 'alae who immediately began to pump his neck and head back and forth. Soon there was the sound of crackling and Māui peeked out of his hiding place to see a fire, flames flickering in the midst of sticks of wood while a plume of white smoke climbed up into the sky. The birds were gathered around this fire, chattering loudly and trying to hasten the cooking of their bananas.

"Let us cook quickly," they chanted, "let us cook quickly. The swift sons of Hina will soon come."

Māui threw back the coverings of vines and leaped out to rush amongst the birds. The eight scattered the fire and stamped out the embers under their webbed feet, squawking loudly as they did. The youngest bird tried to snatch his banana from the coals and flee, but Māui seized him by the neck. He forgot for a moment that he wanted the secret of making fire. He was so angry to have been tricked by these birds that his first impulse was to wring the little bird's neck. "That's for you!" he yelled and twisted the feathery neck.

"Wait!" called the 'alae. "If you kill me, the secret of fire will die too. You will never have fire. You will never have cooked food to eat. Your mother will always curse you!"

Māui paused. His fingers trembled with the desire to continue to choke the bird to death. He looked down at the 'alae and said, "What is the secret, then?"

"You must promise to let me live," the bird replied.

"Of course," said Māui. "I'll spare your life but only if you give me the secret of fire."

The wily bird thought that if she promised to give the secret, Māui would let her go and she could escape without saying anything. But Māui was too wise for that. He sat back on his heels and said, "Give me the secret," but he did not let go of the bird's neck which was a quarter turn twisted in a most uncomfortable manner for the bird.

"Well, you must rub two plants together," the bird said. "Fire will come from that."

"Is that why you pump your head back and forth?" Māui asked. "That is the motion you must make?"

The bird tried to nod its head but Māui's fingers were in the way.

"What two plants are rubbed together?" Māui demanded.

"You must take a stalk of the 'ape plant," the 'alae said, "and put it on the ground. Then take a stalk of the taro plant and rub it over the 'ape stalk. Fire will come."

Māui looked about him and saw both the 'ape and taro stalks near at hand. He gathered them together without letting go of the bird who fluttered its wings in an attempt to get away from Māui. But Māui just tucked the bird firmly under his arm, still keeping hold of its neck in a slight twist. Māui then put down the 'ape stalk and rubbed the taro stalk over it. But both plants are water plants and nothing but water came out.

"This is not right," Māui said. He turned the bird's neck another quarter twist until the bird could no longer look forward but only backwards over its back.

"Wait!" called the bird. "You must use two pieces of banana stump."

Māui saw the bananas roasting and smelled them and he thought this might be a reasonable choice. So, following directions, he rapidly moved the upper stick across the under stick of banana.

The bird's hope for an unguarded moment when he might escape went for nothing for Māui was very careful not to let go. Indeed, after a short while the banana pieces had yielded only water and were useless pulp in his hands and Māui became very angry.

"You are trying to trick me," he growled and twisted the bird's neck another quarter turn.

"Wait!" the bird called desperately. "You're right. There is no fire in green plants. There is fire in dry wood only."

"Which wood?" asked Māui.

And the bird named him a kind of wood. But again and again, Māui got no fire. His hands hurt rubbing the wooden pieces against each other. His hand hurt from holding the bird's neck in a slowly strangling hold.

Each time he tried a different wood, each time he got no fire, each time he twisted the bird's neck a little bit more. The bird was half dead by this time and Māui was really considering giving up the whole thing with a sharp twist to break the bird's neck when the 'alae said, "Try a piece of hau on the ground. Let that be the 'aunaki, the piece of stick rubbed upon. Use a stick of noni for the 'aulima, the stick you hold in your hand."

So Māui put down a piece of hau and tried rubbing a stick from the noni bush across it. Again no fire came but the hau stick was warm to the touch!

"Still not quite right," Māui said and twisted the neck a little bit more.

"Wait!" croaked the 'alae, now having much difficulty breathing. "Now use a piece of olomea for the 'aulima."

So Māui rubbed the hau stick with a piece of olomea. First there was a feeling of warmth, then a little flicker of light, then a small plume of smoke began to rise from the hau stick.

"Quick!" croaked the bird, "pile some amaumau fern against the spark."

Māui threw on some 'āma'uma'u fern and continued rubbing. Suddenly there was a tongue of yellow and red rising from the fern and smoke climbed swiftly into the sky. Māui reached out to touch the tongue of flame and pulled back his fingers with a yell. It hurt!

"There," said the bird, "now you have the secret of fire. Let me go now."

Māui did not let the bird go and continued to stare at the fire. He wasn't quite sure what to do with fire yet, but he thought he would ask his mother Hina-a-ke-ahi about that. She would know how to cook with fire. Hadn't she mentioned several different ways to him?

The bird tried to pull away from the cruel fingers of Māui. "Let me go," she pleaded.

"Not yet," Māui replied. "There is one more thing to rub."

With that, he picked up the burning stick of hau and rubbed it back and forth across the top of the bird's head until all the feathers fell off and raw flesh appeared that quickly became scorched. The odor of burning feathers and flesh made both Māui and the bird cough unhappily. The bird squawked and screamed and struggled but could not break loose.

Finally Māui stopped rubbing the burning stick over the bird's head. He put the bird down in front of him and looked sternly at it. "Now you have a red place on the top of your head," he said, "to remind me that you would not willingly give me the secret of fire so I could give my mother cooked food. You, your friends, and all your descendants will always bear this red mark on your heads to remind you not to trick Māui, son of Hina."

And indeed from that day on the 'alae birds have always carried the scars of fire on their heads.

Māui learned how to draw out the sparks secreted in different kinds of trees. The 'iliahi, the fire-bark or sandalwood tree was one and another was pua, a member of the olive family. Hina taught him how to steam food in an underground oven and how to heat stones before dropping them into calabashes of prepared food, and how to broil over an open fire. He learned that fire kept people warm at night and gave light to tell stories by. Never again did Hina sigh for cooked food, never again did she long for a bowl of fresh poi made from the steamed roots of the taro plant, pounded and mixed with water, for fire brought her this food.

But the 'alae never returned to the fire. Their heads hurt too much. Instead they hunt in the streams where they live and eat what they find there. Only raw food for them!

KA PAIO O ʻŌPAEKAʻA

K e-li'i-koa was very angry. He was the ruling chief of the kingdom of Waimea. He was descended from Ka-hanai-a-ke-akua, the chief who, traveling in his sea-going canoe, was the first to find Kaua'i and had settled the empty land. Ke-li'i-koa was tall, sturdy of body, and an excellent warrior. No woman, he felt, could look once upon him and not be smitten by his appearance. Yet a woman had rejected him, was refusing to marry him.

She was Ka-'ili-lau-o-ke-koa and not only was she as beautiful as her name implied, she was also her father's only child and would some day inherit the kingdom of Wailua. It never entered Ke-li'i-koa's thoughts that perhaps such a woman might have a mind of her own and see no reason to marry the high chief of Kona. Ke-li'i-koa went to Wailua, confident that his position and good looks would immediately overwhelm the young chiefess.

But she was not overwhelmed. She listened to Ke-li'i-koa's proposal and watched him in the various contests of physical strength, of boxing, spear throwing, and wrestling, seeing a man who liked hurting others, who enjoyed humiliating his fallen opponent, who was arrogant when he won, bitterly angry and claiming trickery when he lost. Ka-'ili-lau-o-ke-koa was not impressed.

Instead she chose a chief from upper Wailua. He, Ka-ua-kahi-ali'i and his sister Ka-hale-lehua lived near the heiau of Pihana-ka-lani and were the adopted children of the priestess Waha, the spiritual leader of the seven sacred heiau that stretched from the river mouth to the mountain source. It was said that Waha could control the rains and the thunder and lightning that came with fierce storms.

Ke-li'i-koa returned to his own house after the black tapa which symbolized the marriage of Ka-'ili-lau-o-ke-koa and Ka-ua-kahi-ali'i had covered them, and grumbled to his advisor, cousin, and friend Pi'i-Kalalau. "I'd like to kill them both." He flopped down on his bed and sulked.

Pi'i gauged his mood. Pi'i himself had pointed out the benefits that a marriage of Ke-li'i-koa and Ka-'ili-lau-o-ke-koa would bring, nothing less than the uniting of the entire island under one leader. His family had been advisors to the high chiefs of Kona since that first canoe of settlers had arrived under the leadership of Ka-hanai-a-ke-akua. Beside this young chief had stood the first Pi'i, so fierce and cunning he was said to be part-man, part-lizard and that he could at will take on the appearance of a man, young or aged, a giant, or a mo'o, a lizard of such size and ferocity as to be feared by all.

Pi'i said, "The marriage of Ka-'ili-lau-o-ke-koa and Ka-ua-kahi-ali'i need not last too long."

Ke-li'i-koa sat up like a squid rising toward the baited cowry shell, a smile on his face as the implication struck him. "His life may be short," Ke-li'i-koa suggested.

"Indeed." Pi'i waited. The art of advice is in knowing when silence is most eloquent.

"An accident," Ke-li'i-koa mused.

Pi'i said, "Tomorrow we have been invited to join the married couple surfing the waves of Maka-'iwa."

"So?" sneered Ke-li'i-koa. "I am not good on a surfboard. I am not going."

"No one is better than you at riding the waves in a small outrigger canoe," Pi'i said. "But, of course, you must be careful. A canoe can hurt if it strikes a fallen surfer."

Bidding Ke-li'i-koa good night, Pi'i left his chief to dream his own dreams.

The day of surfing was bright and clear. Maka-'iwa surf ran high with smooth breakers for the sport of chiefs.

Ka-'ili-lau-o-ke-koa was there laughing at the waves for she loved no sport more than surfing. Ka-ua-kahi-ali'i was there, concentrating on the waves for, being mountain bred, he had seldom surfed. He counted on his own physical abilities to keep him from becoming the butt of jokes. Ke-li'i-koa was there in a small outrigger canoe, taking Ka-'ili-lau-o-ke-koa's playful taunts of those who could not ride the waves properly on boards. He took wave after wave with her, she standing, he sitting and whenever Ka-'ili-lau-o-ke-koa paddled out to the breakers, Ke-li'i-koa was near her. She did not realize she was being guided closer and closer toward her husband, the canoe keeping her from heading away to leave Ka-ua-kahi-ali'i to learn on his own. Then Ka-'ili-lau-o-ke-koa and Ka-ua-kahi-ali'i were side by side, a blue green wall of water lifted them and the two rose on their boards and rode the wave. The canoe sped toward Ka-ua-kahi-ali'i, pushed by the wind and waves as well as the urgings of Ke-li'i-koa's paddle.

Onlookers later agreed that Ke-li'i-koa had misjudged his paddle, had dipped it in the ocean like this, no, like that, but no matter, outrigger canoes were not made for surfing and Ke-li'i-koa's went out of control. The canoe crashed into Ka-ua-kahi-ali'i's surfboard. The board, canoe, and man tangled and the wave rushed over them and tumbled them along. Ke-li'i-koa almost shouted aloud with joy as he felt his canoe hit Ka-ua-kahi-ali'i. Ka-ua-kahi-ali'i would now be dead or at least crippled for life.

Ka-'ili-lau-o-ke-koa turned over the crest of the wave, dropped flat on her board and paddled in frantic haste toward the wreckage. Ke-li'i-koa swam to the same spot and the two met just as Ka-ua-kahi-ali'i bobbed to the surface, bruised and bleeding, but not as hurt as Ke-li'i-koa had hoped. Ka-ua-kahi-ali'i looked about and seeing the two anxious faces looking at him, burst into laughter.

"Don't worry," he called. "I'm all right. I know the ways of the ocean. It was just an accident."

But sitting on the beach near a group of boys playing with darts made of sugar cane tassels, Waha had seen the incident. Her eyes flashed with anger. It was no accident she had seen.

Waha called to one of the boys, "See if you can hit that girl with your dart." She pointed to a young woman sitting nearby.

The laughing boy threw his pua, a dart made from the tassel of sugar cane. Unknown to him, Waha guided the pua's flight with her power. The dart flew over the girl's head and flew faster, turning into the wind and aiming for the three people emerging from the sea.

"Watch out!" yelled Waha. Ke-li'i-koa jerked about, startled, to look at the old woman. The blunt end of the dart banged into one of his eyes with enough strength to destroy the eyeball itself.

Ke-li'i-koa with a bellow of pain and rage grabbed up a spear and ran to the group of frightened boys. "Who threw the dart?" the furious chief demanded.

"I did," said the no longer laughing boy, "but. . ."

Ke-li'i-koa thrust his spear through the boy. He was only a commoner's child and no one would revenge his death.

After Ke-li'i-koa had been delivered to the physicians, Waha ordered a proper burial for the boy. "Your journey to Milu, god of the realms of the dead, will be quick," she promised the boy, "and you will be a retainer of Milu himself."

Late that night, after all the physicians had done their best for the damaged eye and the last sympathetic visitor had gone, Pi'i said, "They don't suspect. All think it was an accident."

"Yes, caused by my lack of skill," Ke-li'i-koa raged. "Everyone thinks I'm a fool and deserve no better than to lose an eye. If they only knew!"

Pi'i nodded. "Yes, you did well. However Ka-ua-kahi-ali'i was not badly hurt. Any other man would be dead. His aumakua, his guardian spirits, guard him well."

"The mo'o and the owl are my aumakua," Ke-li'i-koa said. "Where is their help? I have lost an eye."

"They are here," Pi'i said. "However you can't be involved in another accident. Once an accident, twice a suspicion. No, leave this to me. You will have a fever, your accident today leaves you with no choice. You will return to Waimea. I will remain."

In these words, Ke-li'i-koa read a torrent of meanings. He nodded to show he understood and fell asleep.

Ke-li'i-koa, suffering from a fever, was carried off to Waimea and Pi'i remained to do the honors of his kingdom. He held a great feast and brought dancers to entertain his guests and chanters to sing stories of the ancient days. Pi'i did all he could to amuse the young chief Ka-ua-kahi-ali'i and to be friendly. As the days went past, Pi'i became an inseparable companion, so much so that a faint suspicion was born in Ka-'ili-lau-o-ke-koa's thoughts. Why was Pi'i quite so friendly? Why did the friendliness seem false? His eyes seemed cunning and wary to her. Why was she reminded of the kōlea, the bird that came to Kaua'i thin and hungry, remained to eat and grow fat and then leave again? They took all and returned nothing. Pi'i was like that, Ka-'ili-lau-o-ke-koa thought. He professed great friendship but, she sensed, he really didn't mean it. She grew suspicious of him.

Another pair of eyes watched and speculated, the dark eyes of a white-haired woman who never seemed part of any occasion but was always there. Pi'i never noticed her.

After several weeks had passed, Pi'i invited Ka-ua-kahi-ali'i to visit him at his house. It was the night of the full moon and from the doorway there was a superb view of 'Ōpaeka'a waterfall. In the moonlight, Pi'i said, one could see the shrimp rolling about in the waterfall. Ka-ua-kahi-ali'i accepted for he had not seen all there was to be seen on Kaua'i and was curious and eager.

Ka-'ili-lau-o-ke-koa however had grown up within sight of 'Ōpaeka'a falls. She had never heard of such a special spectacle by moonlight. She wondered why Pi'i had offered her new husband a lie but said nothing. But, when Ka-ua-kahi-ali'i and Pi'i went along to the path to 'Ōpaeka'a, Ka-'ili-lau-o-ke-koa and a small group of warriors followed silently.

Pi'i and Ka-ua-kahi-ali'i laughed and chatted as they strolled along. The moon turned the trees and rocks around them to the color of clean wood ashes. The rumbling of the falls echoed from the cliff walls. At a bend of the stream, Pi'i pointed out a house.

"Enter. Come in," Pi'i invited. "We will have some 'awa and watch the spectacle of 'Ōpaeka'a falls." Pi'i ducked down and entered the house through the low doorway. "Come in and sit down."

Ka-ua-kahi-ali'i too stooped down and began to enter the doorway. An unexpected movement alerted him and he ducked his head to one side. Something heavy crashed against his shoulder and Ka-ua-kahi-ali'i felt some bones break. With pain and anger, Ka-ua-kahi-ali'i jumped backwards, tripped, and fell on his back. A huge figure leaped through the doorway after him and attempted to pierce Ka-ua-kahi-ali'i through the chest with a long barbed kauila spear. Ka-ua-kahi-ali'i, in spite of his broken shoulder bones, was so well trained in the practice of spears that he managed to avoid the thrust. His arm dangling uselessly, Ka-ua-kahi-ali'i could only dodge and parry the thrusts and quickly tired.

Ka-'ili-lau-o-ke-koa, coming up at that moment, saw her husband slip and fall to one knee. Picking up a rock, she seated it in her sling, twirled it above her head and let fly. The rock hit the huge figure on one eye. The giant bellowed and clapped his head.

Ka-‘ili-lau-o-ke-koa fired off another stone which struck the giant on his chest. The giant fell backwards. Ka-‘ili-lau-o-ke-koa ran to her husband and helped him to his feet and the two of them ran as fast as they could into the safety of the sacred coconut grove.

When they arrived home, Ka-‘ili-lau-o-ke-koa ordered her warriors to stand guard and sent one of them to tell Waha her services were needed.

The white-haired woman with watchful eyes came and set her foster son's broken bones. She wrapped a poultice of crushed noni fruit about his shoulder as she asked, "Who attacked you?"

"I don't know," Ka-ua-kahi-ali‘i said. "I only watched the spear tip so I could avoid it. I did not see who was behind it."

"It was a tall man, taller than Ka-ua-kahi-ali‘i," Ka-‘ili-lau-o-ke-koa said. "He had large shiny eyes that gleamed in the moonlight, so I aimed for them. I've never seen such a creature before."

"And where is Pi‘i?" Waha asked.

Ka-ua-kahi-ali‘i and Ka-‘ili-lau-o-ke-koa shook their heads. Neither of them knew.

Waha smiled grimly. "Stay with Ka-ua-kahi-ali‘i," she told Ka-‘ili-lau-o-ke-koa. "Protect him if you must." The old woman strode from the house.

"Bring all the warriors here in Wailua to me," she told her attendant. When they were gathered, Waha led them through the coconut grove to the house of Pi‘i. She ordered the house surrounded.

"Pi‘i!" she called. "Your treachery is known to me. Come out!"

In answer, Pi‘i rushed from his house. Later the warriors, recounting their story, agreed he was at least twelve feet tall. He had hair as red as flames, shining white eyes as large as a man's fist, a mouth full of tusks, and legs like young trees. Waha was not deceived. As Pi‘i paused in his doorway, she saw he was wearing a tall helmet. On a wicker framework, there had been created a face with pig tusks lining its mouth, shiny eyes of mother-of-pearl, and red tail feathers from wild roosters. This was the sacred helmet of the mo‘o, the great lizards who had once roamed the ancestral homelands far to the west. But those who claimed the mo‘o as their guardians were powerful and to be feared.

Pi'i-Kalalau gave his battle cry, a fearsome hiss, and killed the nearest warrior with a kick in the stomach and speared the second man with his barbed spear. Pi'i lunged at the rest of the warriors who fled as the giant mo'o charged them. Waha uttered her war cry, a shrill bird call of defiance. She caught up her ikoi, a heavy piece of wood tied to a long strong cord of coconut fiber. She twirled it above her head and let it go. It flew and wrapped itself around Pi'i, binding his arms to his side.

"Kill him!" Waha ordered.

The warriors rushed upon him, showering him with stones and poking him with their spears. Pi'i forced the coconut fibers and with a thrust of his arms the cord broke. Once again he drove the warriors before him, intending this time to reach the house of Ka-ua-kahi-ali'i and kill him once and for all.

Waha raised her arms, her hands and fingers shaping the words of her prayer, sending them to the gods:

> Born is the night,
> Born is the morning,
> Born is the thunder,
> Born is the lightning,
> Born is the heavy rain,
> Born is the rain which I summon.
> The clouds of the sky gather!
> Lono-i-ka-'ou-ali'i,
> Let the lightning flash!

So powerful was her prayer that a cloud, towering and flat topped, appeared above the scene of conflict. Deep rumblings vibrated the air and a shaft of lightning flashed from the cloud and burnt the ground in front of Pi'i, almost overwhelming him.

Waha's voice seemed rolled into the thunder. "Pi'i-Kalalau! Your treachery is repaid!"

A second flash of lightning blinded and stunned Pi'i. He knew now that he was dealing with a priestly power, but he too was a priest. He, too, could pray for help.

Owl of the high mountains,
Owl of the sea shore,
Ruler of all the birds,
Of all feathered creatures,
Fly from Nā Molokama!
The lightning burns!

Pi'i dodged the fiery bolts of lightning as best he could but some fell so near him he was close to death. Then a huge owl flew down from his mountain home and hovered over Pi'i's head. Whenever Waha hurled a fiery dart, the owl swiftly thrust his head from side to side and caught it in his beak. With a shake of his head, he tossed it aside where it fell harmlessly to the ground. Pi'i, stunned by lightning and reverberating thunder, stood unmoving.

Waha ordered the warriors to attack. The warriors threw their spears and hurled rocks into the storm. A huge cloud of rocks struck both the owl and the lizard until both were bleeding and bruised. Waha's lightning came so quickly the eye only saw a sheet of flaming light.

Pi'i, unable to withstand the assault, cried out to his owl guardian, "Fly! Back to the mountains. There will be another time!"

The owl caught a last bolt of lightning in its beak. He launched himself towards Waha and shook the lightning free. It struck at Waha's feet, causing her to recoil. Her concentration broken, the storm she controlled diminished. The warriors formed a protective screen around the sorceress as the owl flew back into the mountains to nurse its burned beak and bleeding wounds.

Pi'i turned and ran upstream and clambered up the face of the waterfall. Hand over hand, from fingerhold to toehold, he fled toward Hanalei valley, seeking the safety of his home in Kalalau. Later the Wailua warriors all agreed that he had changed into a huge lizard which scampered up the pali with incredible speed, frightened of course by the showers of stones they had thrown.

The warriors returned to tell their tale and Ka-'ili-lau-o-ke-koa nursed her husband. Waha, with her attendant, followed Pi'i and on a small ridge in the center of Hanalei valley, she caught up to the treacherous man and killed him.

Then tired and depleted of energy, Waha returned to Pihana-ka-lani to rest and wait. Pi'i-Kalalau was gone, but Ke-li'i-koa, ruling chief of Kona, was still angry.

HINA-HAU-KAEKAE

ina-hau-kaekae listened sadly to the shouting, to the paddling of bare feet hurrying from one place to another, to all the sounds of preparation for the special day ahead. Hina-hau-kaekae knew she would have no part in this day and she was sad. She so wanted to be helpful, to be useful to people. She did what she could within the tall walls of Malae heiau where she lived and did certainly as much as her sister allowed her to do. Her sister Hina-puku-i'a would never allow her to leave the heiau walls except to visit their other sister, Hina-puku-'ai, who lived at Poli'ahu heiau across the river and up the hill.

Hina-puku-i'a knew all the secrets of gathering food from the sea, how to weave funnel-mouthed fishtraps to catch the shy hīnālea, how to use a cowry shell to lure octopus, how to gather edible seaweed, all this and so much more Hina-pupu-i'a knew. And Hina-kupu-'ai kept busy too for she knew all the secrets of gathering food from the land, how to plant taro in irrigated fields, how to grow bananas so the fruit would be heavy, how to recognize which wild berries were safe to eat and which were not, and so much more. The sisters taught these skills as they moved from island to island across the deep sea.

Hina-hau-kaekae had begged her sisters to let her help. But when Hina-kupu-i'a asked, "What can you do?" she couldn't answer for she had no skills.

"Why must I live as a prisoner inside a heiau's walls?" asked Hina-hau-kaekae. "What does it matter where I live? I'm no use to anyone."

Hina-kupu-i'a replied, "When we left our home, our mother made us promise that you would be on sacred ground before the sun sets and that you would not leave until after the sun rises."

"She gave me this flower," Hina-hau-kaekae protested, "so I could be outside during the day." She held out the large five-petaled flower cupped in her hands. Early in the morning its petals were pale yellow. As the day progressed, the flower changed color, becoming darker and darker until, by the end of the day, it was a dull red. By observing the changing color of this flower, Hina-hau-kaekae would know the time of day.

"But you never look at it," her sister said. "Several times night has almost caught you outside. We have so much to do we must leave before dawn and return after sunset. It's easier for us to keep you inside the sacred enclosure at all times."

So once again this morning, Hina-hau-kaekae lay on her bed and listened, bored and unhappy. After a time, the sounds died away and she got up. She called but no one answered. Another day with no one to talk to, another day of loneliness. She climbed to the top of the heiau wall. The heiau itself was on the rise of a hill. To the north the ground fell steeply to the banks of the Wailua river. On the east the land sloped down to the sea and grassy plains on the north stretched to Hanamā'ulu. Across the river, hills humped up and down like a lizard's back and on the highest point she could see the heiau of Poli'ahu where her sister Hina-kupu-'ai lived. She looked toward the sea. All along the reef were men with round nets practicing their throws and women were gathering seaweed. She looked again toward Poli'ahu. It would be easy, she thought, to cross the river and climb the hills to Poli'ahu to visit her sister. There would be plenty of time before the sun set.

As she walked down to the bank of the Wailua, she met a boy and a girl. The boy was holding a square flat object she had never seen before. It was made of tree branches lashed together and covered with a colorful piece of old tapa. One end of a string was tied to a crosspiece and the other end was held by the girl. The girl began running and when the string was pulled tight, the boy threw the contraption high into the wind. It soared into the sky, tugging against the string, and almost flew, but then it faltered and crashed to earth.

Hina-hau-kaekae kneeled next to the children as they looked unhappily at the broken bits of wood and tapa.

"What is this thing that wants to fly but can't?" she asked.

"It's a kite," the girl said. "My grandfather told us about kites and how they fly in the sky. He saw them in Kahiki before he came here to Kaua'i in the long canoes."

"But the wood is too heavy," the boy said. "We've tried branches from every tree on the island and they're all too heavy."

"We need a lightweight wood," the girl said, "strong and light. Then maybe our kite would fly."

Hina-hau-kaekae wanted to help them. "I know of such a tree," she whispered, trying to remember when and where she had heard of it.

"Where?" the boy asked eagerly.

"Which one?" the girl asked. The two children had spoken as one.

Hina-hau-kaekae shook her head. "I haven't seen it today," she said. "I'm a stranger to Kaua'i. But as I walk along today, I'll look out for it and when I find it, I'll let you know." In her mind's eye she could see this tree that had tough supple branches yet was very light. She couldn't remember ever having seen this tree yet she knew it existed.

She left the children and walked down to the river. In Malae heiau where she had forgotten it, the flower her mother had given her darkened.

When she got to the river bank she joined a group of people preparing a long square-cornered net. Some women were sitting on the grass mending the net, their fingers tying knots as the shuttles sped through the mesh like birds startled from rest. Some men were tying wooden floats onto the top edge of the net, while still others tied ti leaf bundles to the bottom that would act as brooms sweeping the river bottom to scare the fish up into the net. Hina-hau-kaekae sat among the women, watching eagerly. She wanted to help but had no skills that were useful to these tasks. At least, she thought, she could hold onto one end of the net when it was stretched across the river.

In time, one end was anchored to the shore and the rest of the net was piled high in a canoe. The unsteady canoe was slowly paddled across the river and the net was played out until it stretched from one shore to the other. For a short time the net floated but the wooden floats were not buoyant and the net sank into the depths of the water. Everyone groaned. The far end of the net was brought back and the entire net hauled ashore. The catch was meager for most fish had swum over the top of the net and only a few were caught in the meshes.

Hina-hau-kaekae, remembering the kite fliers, said, "The wood floats are too heavy."

The head fisherman agreed. "Much too heavy. But this is the lightest wood there is on the island. We've tried everything. What we need is a tree with good sized branches, light, that won't sink, and is easily hollowed out. But, of course, no such tree exists."

A shiver of recognition tickled Hina-hau-kaekae's back. "Such a tree exists somewhere," she said. "I know that but I don't know where it is. I'll look for it as I walk along today and when I find it, I'll let you know."

"We'd thank you every time our nets floated," the head fisherman said.

Hina-hau-kaekae left the fisherfolk and continued downstream to find a place to cross over. In Malae heiau where she had forgotten it, the flower turned bright yellow, the richness of the sun at mid-morning.

Soon Hina-hau-kaekae saw that the river flowed into the ocean, an angry meeting of the rain waters of Wai'ale'ale and the surf of Maka'iwa. There was no place she could ford the river on foot.

She came upon a man who was tying curved branches between his canoe and a log. "This is an outrigger," he explained, answering Hina-hau-kaekae's question. "It should balance the weight of the canoe so it will be steady on the water yet remain easy enough for one man to handle."

"I'd like a ride in your canoe," she asked.

"Let me take you across the river," he replied. "Can you swim? The outrigger has never really worked. The idea is good, I think, but something's wrong."

"I can swim and perhaps I'll see what's wrong," she answered.

They climbed into the canoe and had to sit very carefully. Sometimes the outrigger soared into the air and they had to throw themselves onto the crossbeams to push the floating beam back into the water. When they did that, the outrigger began to sink until they threw themselves to the other side of the canoe to force the beam back up to the surface. It was a short ride but both man and passenger were exhausted when they reached shore.

"Do you see what's wrong?" the man asked.

"The outrigger is too heavy."

The man thought a bit. "I see," he said. "The float should be lightweight and somewhat curved. That way the weight would remain equal and not shift from canoe to outrigger. A tree with wood like that doesn't grow on Kaua'i because I've looked."

Hina-hau-kaekae's skin tingled with goosebumps. "I know such a tree grows," she said, "and I'm looking for it."

Hina-hau-kaekae wandered along the river bank through a grove of coconut trees. In Malae heiau the forgotten flower blazed the brilliant yellow of the sun directly overhead. It was cool under the shade of the coconut trees and she gave no thought to the sun which caused the shadows. As she walked, she kept looking for this special tree. It would be a tree, she thought, that would be very helpful to kites, to hukilau nets, to outrigger canoes. Happy to be helping people, she searched high and low, forgetting the reason she had left Malae that morning.

She came upon a woman sitting on the grass who was crying and from time to time shaking with a dry hacking cough. It was an ugly sound, an effort to clear phlegm that was too deep and dry to be coughed up.

Hina-hau-kaekae hurried to her and massaged the back of the woman's neck and gently soothed the front of her throat where she could feel the Adam's apple jerk and contract with each hacking cough.

"You mustn't cry," Hina-hau-kaekae said. "It won't help your cough."

"I'm not crying for myself," the woman said. "I should be with my sister who is at Holoholo-kū heiau, just over there, waiting for her baby to be born. The baby does not want to come and my sister is very tired. She couldn't stand my coughing and sent me away."

"There must be some medicines that would help," Hina-hau-kaekae said.

The woman shook her head. "No," she said. "I've studied all the plants that grow on Kaua'i. There's nothing to help a mother give birth nor give quick relief to a cough like mine."

Hina-hau-kaekae's skin crawled with gooseflesh. "Yes, there's such a plant that will give you these two medicines and more besides," she said.

"Which one? Where is it?" the woman asked quickly.

"I don't know its name or where it is," Hina-hau-kaekae admitted. "It grows, that I do know. When I find it, I'll show it to you."

"You'd be remembered and thanked each time the medicine was used," the woman said.

Hina-hau-kaekae continued her journey to Poli'ahu. In Malae, there was now a blush of orange on the forgotten flower. She came to where ʻŌpae-kaʻa stream enters the Wailua river. There were only two hills to climb before she would be at journey's end. As she was about to cross the stream, three people came down the path toward her.

There was a bright-eyed white-haired woman in the lead. She was holding a precarious collection of gourd containers in her arms. Behind her marched two young men, one of them as quick-moving as a forest bird, the other as slow and steady as a great sea bird. Both of them, too, were carrying a large collection of gourd containers whose roundness made them extremely difficult to hold together.

One of the gourds in the woman's arms suddenly seemed to sprout wings and flew up out of her arms and fell to the ground. The lid popped open and tiny red feathers floated out.

"Quick, get the feathers!" yelled the old woman.

All three put down the gourds and scrambled after the feathers. Hina-hau-kaekae ran from one place to another catching a feather in the air here, from a blade of grass there, until they'd all been returned to the gourd and the lid firmly tied into place.

"You need a net bag to hold all these things," Hina-hau-kaekae said.

"So we do," the old woman answered. "My grandsons here are birdcatchers and I make feather lei, so we always have lots to carry. At the beach, one can make net bags at the last minute out of pōhuehue vines, but we live in the mountains and there the only thing for nets is olonā but I use all the olonā, which is not easy to get, to make the backing of the capes and helmets I make, as well as the string I use to tie the feathers on. There are no other plants that one can use to make nets on Kauaʻi. Such nets would be very useful and I wish there was a tree whose bark we could use."

"Such a net must be quick and easy to make," the tall forest man said. "The bark must be soft and supple."

"It must be strong," the slower, bigger grandson said. "As the bark dries, it must remain strong and not become brittle and break."

"And of course there's no such tree," the old woman sighed. "Pick up the gourds, we must be off."

The three walked on, their arms filled to overflowing with their bundles and gourds. Hina-hau-kaekae felt her skin tingle as though something strange were about to happen. "There is such a tree, with so much bark you could never use it all!" she called to the birdcatchers. "I know there is!"

Hina-hau-kaekae walked slowly along the path. Behind her, at Malae, the flower was now a dull red, but the lonely young woman did not know that. Beside her the grasses on the hill grew still as the ocean breeze died away. The river's water darkened as the sun sat on the top of Wai'ale'ale for a brief rest before continuing on. Behind her, the sky turned a deep blue and the first sparkling eyes of heaven looked down on Kaua'i.

Hina-hau-kaekae reached the foot of the steep hill that rose to Poli'ahu heiau. She knew she must hurry now and reach there before the sun was gone. She had to be on sacred ground before nightfall. She stepped out on the right foot, but then she turned to look back. She had not found the tree she knew existed somewhere. Her promises were not kept. She remembered the children with their kite and she pointed toward them with her right arm. There were the fisherfolk who needed floats and she gestured toward their place. There was the man with the outrigger canoe and the coughing woman and she gestured toward them, seeking forgiveness for not having helped them. She looked down the trail where she had met the birdcatchers, she looked up at Poli'ahu, she looked up at the stars. So many promises, and none kept. She wanted to turn back to help, she wanted to run up the hill to the heiau. She could not decide what to do and stood turning this way and that.

She shivered and her skin turned dark and rough. Her feet sent down roots and anchored her to the ground. Her fingers sent out small branches that put forth leaves and buds and flowers. Her small branches were just right to make a kite that soars into the sky to talk to passing clouds. The thicker branches would make floats that hold the top of hukilau nets at water level so few fish can escape. The trunk of this tree, arched and light, would be ideal for an outrigger balancing the weight of a canoe. The flower buds when chewed would clear the throat of dry phlegm and the soft slimy scrapings from the trunk would help mothers deliver their babies more easily. The bark, sliced into strips, would weave quickly into carrying nets that become stronger as the bark dried.

Hina-hau-kaekae herself was the tree for which she searched that day, the tree of

Hina-hau-kaekae, the hau. The place where she stopped undecided, gesturing here and there, looking up and down, all tangled and confused — the way a hau grows even today — this place was named Hina-a-ka-lāhau, The-place-where-the-hau-leaves-spread.

The flowers of the hau still mark the passage of time. At dawn the flower opens and is a pale yellow. By noon, the flower has become a deep yellow, bright and fierce as the sun itself. At dusk the flower is as deep a red as the sunset. This was the warning to Hina-hau-kaekae that the day was passing. Perhaps she is happier as she is, helpful to all who use her, than living in a heiau forgotten by all.

PAKA‘A

aka'a lived with his mother La'amaomao and his uncle Mailou the birdcatcher in a small house on the cliffs of Ke-ahiahi that lie between Kapa'a and Ke'alia.

Boys his own age teased him about his uncle Mailou who was so short many thought he was a dwarf. He was an excellent birdcatcher and for the bundles of red, green, and yellow feathers he brought back to Chief Pai'ea he was given taro from the royal farms and fish caught by the royal fishermen. Sometimes he brought back a bunch of bananas he'd found growing wild or a container full of fresh water shrimp from the mountain streams. Paka'a and his mother La'amaomao were never hungry for Mailou took good care of them.

Sometimes on calm days Mailou pulled his canoe from the storage shed and pushed it across the sand into the sea. Then boy and uncle spent the day fishing on the outer edges of the reef. Because of these days Paka'a never went with his uncle into the mountains. Paka'a's heart belonged to the sea.

He spent hours lying on his stomach under the hala trees at Ke-ahiahi watching Chief Pai'ea's fishermen, even if all he could see were little dots on the horizon as they fished in the deep sea grounds.

Whenever the fishermen returned from an expedition to catch mālolo, the blue flying fish, Paka'a would hurry to the shore to help them unload in the hopes they would give him some to take home. Mālolo was his favorite eating fish. He liked it raw, mixed with līpoa seaweed. Best of all he loved mālolo wrapped in ti leaves and baked in the underground oven. But the fishermen would open-handedly share their catch with everyone but Paka'a. To him they gave only one or two damaged mālolo and called him names.

One day he walked home with only one fish which he gave to his mother. His heart was heavy and tears trembled at the edge of his eyes. "Why do they give me only one small mālolo when everyone else walked away with one in each hand?" he asked La'amaomao.

La'amaomao replied, "The fishermen think your uncle Mailou is lazy because he spends all his time catching birds in the mountains."

"Chief Pai'ea sends him there," Paka'a said, "just as he sends the head fishermen with his men to sea. All work for the High Chief."

"Yes, they do," La'amaomao said.

"But the fishermen can give them to whom they wish."

"After the chief gets his share, that is true," La'amaomao said. "But fishermen like to bet. Maybe if you can't catch mālolo, you can win them!" And La'amaomao laughed and hugged her son with great affection.

But her words remained stuck in Paka'a's ears. There is more than one way to catch a fish, he thought, for he was a lively, curious, observant boy, full of questions he needed to have answered.

Paka'a watched the fishermen and noticed how difficult it was to paddle the canoes out to the deep sea grounds, even with eight paddlers aboard. He sat under the hala trees on the point of Ke-ahiahi, the waves breaking at his feet and watched the fishermen launch their canoes and paddle through the winding channel through the reef and struggle out over the breakers into the open sea.

Going out was bad enough but coming back was worse for the canoes were heavy with fish and the paddlers were tired. If the sea was running high, the channel through the reef was hard to find and many canoes had been overturned and the day's work eaten by the sharks.

One day, as he sat in his grove of hala trees, the retinue of two young chiefs came to the beach at Kapa'a and launched a kite into the air for their amusement. Paka'a stared at the fragile thing of sticks covered with tapa cloth that billowed into the air, the tapa stretched taut in it supports by the wind. Just then, he noticed a flickering out of the corner of his eye and below him on the black rocks a large pai'ea crab scurried out of view. Paka'a hurried down after it but the crab waved its claw threateningly into the air. Paka'a stared at the claw, studied the kite flying high in the air, felt the wind blowing through his hair, and saw the eight-man canoes struggling back toward shore. Paka'a smiled. He had an idea. If it worked he would bet with the fishermen and have all the mālolo he could eat.

He found and cut two slender straight sticks nine feet in length. He cut a notch just above the end of one stick and, seating the other stick into the notch, lashed the two together with olonā cord his uncle had given him. Then he asked his mother for some rolls of lauhala strips and wove a fine-meshed small square net. When he set up this contraption, pushing the upright stick into the sand, the wind blew against the mat which billowed and ballooned and Paka'a with all his strength could not push against the mat on the downwind side. The whole thing looked like a giant crab claw and perhaps, Paka'a thought, if he set this sail up on his uncle's canoe, the wind would push him and his shoulders would not ache from paddling his canoe. And if it were a good windy day, he ought to be able to go faster than a large canoe with eight men in it.

When Mailou returned at dusk with his catch of birds, Paka'a asked permission to accompany the fishermen on their next trip.

"I might be able to catch forty mālolo myself," he said.

"Small as you are, do you think you could do that?" his mother asked. "You might get drowned."

"I know how to swim," Paka'a assured his mother.

"Look here," said Mailou, "we have all the birds we can eat and sometimes a few mālolo come our way. Isn't that enough?"

"Maybe I can get some sets of fours for ourselves," Paka'a said, his eyes flashing with excitement. "That's better than the scraps we get from the fishermen now."

"What a persistent boy you are," La'amaomao said. "Tomorrow, then, go out fishing for us. Perhaps you can catch four, you stubborn child."

"I could," Paka'a said, "provided you ask my uncle to help me launch his canoe."

"You want to use my canoe?" Mailou asked. "Well, why not?"

The sun had not yet climbed out of the sea to chase away the dark when Mailou carried his outrigger canoe to the edge of the beach. Paka'a trudged behind, a strange bundle of lauhala mat over his shoulder. He stood the bundle upright in the canoe and began to lash it to the outrigger crosspiece at the front of the canoe.

"What is that thing?" Mailou asked. "What are you doing? What mischief are you planning now?"

Paka'a laughed. "Wait and see," he said. When he was done tying the the upright securely to the canoe, he opened the loose stick and the early morning breeze filled the mat.

"What is that?" Mailou asked in astonishment.

"It is a sail," Paka'a said. "With it, if I'm right, I can go faster than any fisherman's canoe."

"The fishermen will laugh at you if you go fishing with such a silly looking thing. It doesn't know whether it is a mat or a crab's claw or a sail, whatever a sail is."

"Let's try it," Paka'a said. Mailou shrugged his shoulders. At best, if nothing happened, he could tease his nephew on his crazy ideas. At worst, he wouldn't mind a swim when the canoe tipped over.

The two pushed the canoe into the water and climbed in. Paka'a pushed out the boom and the breeze filled the sail and the canoe flew over the water as easily as the mālolo skim the waves. Paka'a used a paddle to steer the canoe and it glided through the water and over the coral heads on the reef like a living thing.

Mailou laughed with joy and hugged Paka'a. "I have a smart nephew," he said. "I'm proud of you."

"Do you think I can go fishing now?" Paka'a asked.

"Yes. Go now." Mailou dove overboard and swam to shore.

Paka'a tied up the boom and laid his sail in the bottom of the canoe. He paddled to the landing at Kolokolo where the fishermen were gathering and asked permission to go fishing with them.

Ka-leho, the head fisherman whose legs were crooked from years of twisting them around the large gourd calabash that contained all his equipment, laughed when Paka'a asked to join the fishing fleet. "You are too little to keep up," he said. "You will not get beyond the reef."

Then Ka-leho forgot about the boy completely. He climbed into his canoe and led his fleet beyond the reef. He did not notice Paka'a following them, paddling as fast as he could to keep up.

After a while, Ka-leho looked back at the land and saw that on one side Ke-ahiahi point and the village of Ke-kau-onohi were lined up one above the other while on the other side the mountain trail to Paʻa was just visible over Kalepa hill and knew that he had reached the deep sea fishing ground of Ka-lae-loa-lalo where the mālolo could often be found. Ka-leho brought two eight-man canoes together and each canoe took hold of one end of a long rectangular small-meshed net that was heaped in his canoe and paddled away until the net stretched a hundred feet from canoe to canoe, its upper part just above the surface of the ocean. The rest of the fleet bobbed up and down inside the net circle.

Pakaʻa's canoe was in the middle of the fleet. He soon saw that the men on the outside nearest the net got the fish that were tangled in the meshes and so he paddled to the outside. The older men called to him that his place was not there but he went on lifting up the net like they did and got many of the winged mālolo. He kept dodging about until he had secured as many as he could.

Then the net was gathered into Ka-leho's canoe and the day's fishing was done.

When all was ready to return to shore, Pakaʻa yelled out, "Who will race me back to shore?"

No one answered for the fishermen were amazed at the boldness of this boy that had been a bother and a nuisance all day long.

"Let's have a canoe race," Pakaʻa continued. "If I beat you, your fish will be mine. If you beat me, my fish will be yours."

There was still no answer from the surprised fishermen.

"You can see I'm just a boy," Pakaʻa teased, hoping to anger someone enough to take up his bet, "while you are full grown men. You've no reason to be afraid of me."

Then a large man in a single canoe accepted the challenge. "I'll race you," he said, "if only to shut your silly mouth. That's what comes of having no father to raise you properly."

Pakaʻa flushed but refused to allow himself to get angry. "How many fish do you have?" he asked. "Eight," replied the man.

Pakaʻa replied, "I won't bet with you then. You don't have enough fish. You've only got two times four and I've got two times forty."

Then the steersman of an eight-man canoe spoke up. "Do you care if we bet? There are eight of us and if each of us contribute ten fish, that will match your two forties."

Paka'a saw that all eight men were young, broad shouldered, and that the muscles on their backs were barely covered by their skins. Paka'a's heart leaped with pleasure. These were the fishermen who had teased him most. Their defeat would be very pleasant.

"That depends on whether you have all agreed to the race," said Paka'a.

"We accept your challenge," the eight paddlers replied.

Paka'a then said, "Put your fish in my canoe."

The men laughed. "You'll tip over and lose our fish in the sea. It's better we hold the stakes in our canoe."

Paka'a turned to Ka-leho and said, "You can see that I don't have the strength to resist eight men when they claim the fish if I lose, but if I win they can keep the fish from me when I come for them."

Ka-leho said, "The boy is right. Besides four forties of fish will weigh his canoe down. You have little to fear."

"Agreed," they answered and counted the correct number of mālolo into his canoe. They laughed and teased for they smelled an easy victory. How could one boastful boy beat eight seasoned fishermen?

When all was ready, Ka-leho gave the signal to start. The eight men dug their paddles deep into the sea again and again, the long canoe picked up speed and the canoe hissed its way toward the distant shore. The paddlers looked back and saw to their amazement that Paka'a's canoe was headed in another direction instead of following them. The boy was busy in his canoe and, having stowed the fish carefully to balance his craft, was setting up two sticks to which was tied a lauhala mat.

The eight paddlers laughed, upsetting the rhythm of their own paddling. "Are you hot?" one paddler called.

"Sun too much?"

"Keep our fish cool! Sprinkle water over them!"

Paka'a paid little attention to their words. He saw that they were laughing, their paddles not dipping into the sea as deeply, the steersman no longer paying attention to the catch of the swells that would push them toward shore.

Then Paka'a stepped the boom to spread the sail and paddled backwards to turn the canoe so the wind would fill his crab-claw net.

When the paddlers saw this billowing lauhala mat, they laughed even louder and they did not notice that their canoe slowed.

Ka-leho was watching and, with the suddenness of a rogue wave that overturns unwary canoes, he realized what Paka'a had done. He lifted his hand to signal to his fishermen, but let it drop again. The boy, he thought, had earned his chance. Let him have it.

By this time the eight-man canoe was almost out of sight but as soon as Paka'a had hoisted his sail, he turned his canoe toward land. The wind filled the sail and the canoe skimmed over the deep sea. He sat still, using his paddle as a rudder, guiding his swiftly sailing canoe.

Soon he neared the large boat and the fishermen began to paddle with all their strength. They were no longer laughing as the little outrigger canoe sailed quickly past them. As he passed the large canoe Paka'a chanted:

> The sea swells and rolls,
> A wave that rises and falls but does not break.
> My canoe rides the long backed billow,
> The billows that follow one after another.
> The spray files up from the prow,
> My prow aims at the land.
> Pushed by the breeze Ke-hau.
> The breath of Malamalama-iki,
> Blows my crab-claw sail.
> Say! Where are you?
> Paddles flash in the sun,
> The reflection scared the mālolo of Ka-lae-loa-lalo.
> Who shall be first to the sands of Kolokolo?

The two canoes were almost on the reef. The large canoe slowed to enter the channel but Paka'a skimmed across the reef and beached his canoe on the dry land long before the eight men. The one hundred sixty mālolo were his!

Paka'a shared some of his mālolo with the people who had crowded around to look at the strange sail, the first that had ever been seen in Hawai'i, and to exclaim at his cleverness at being the first to make one. After a time, Paka'a rolled up the sail, put his mālolo in a bag and hurried home to tell his mother and uncle of his good fortune.

La'amaomao's happiness was very great and she said to her son, "I'm rewarded for my care of you. You bring life to my bones."

Mailou was no less happy and it was a very cheerful family which that night for the first time had all the delicious mālolo they could possibly eat.

HŌ MAI KA WAʻA

CHRISTINE FAYE 91

Many years ago, Chief Kualu-nui-pauku-mokumoku brought the Menehune people to Kaua'i. These short, strong people immediately set out to explore their new homeland, searching for the perfect place for their favorite sport. They were searching for a headland that jutted out over the rocks where a diver could easily jump into deep clear ocean water, even on a night lit only by the stars and a crescent moon.

A Menehune diver would stand at the edge of the headland, watching the waves splashing over the rocks below. Beside him would be a pile of round water-polished stones gathered from stream beds. At the proper time between waves, the Menehune would throw a stone far out into the ocean, jump in, catch the stone, and return it to land. The most skillful diver could jump into the waves without making a splash and catch each rock long before it could sink out of sight in the depths of the ocean.

Not all the Menehune were so skillful and many divers returned to shore empty-handed to be teased loudly by his friends. One by one each Menehune would leap feet first after these stones until all of the fresh-water rocks had been lost. This might take several nights but the Menehune were in no rush and swam and dove and gathered food and explored and named certain places after themselves and their adventures.

At last the Menehune came to the mouth of a small valley between Ke'alia and Anahola. A small stream flowed through the valley and crossed a narrow beach before joining the green sea. At one end of the beach was a headland that seemed perfect for their favorite sport. Soon, after beaching their canoe above wave's reach, the Menehune were throwing rocks into the ocean and jumping after them, laughing and shouting so loudly that they scared the 'a'o shearwater birds nesting in burrows along the headland.

Then it was the turn of 'A'aka who, like the others, was broad shouldered, muscular, very short, and very strong. He was named 'A'aka because he was a cranky, crabby person and always complained when it came time to do anything but swim. 'A'aka threw a stone into the water, jumped in, keeping his feet close together so he would not splash any water as he entered, and caught the stone. As he turned to push to the surface, a huge shark, its sharp teeth shining in the green water, lunged for the little man. The shark was ten times bigger than the Menehune so, when 'A'aka changed direction abruptly and fled for the rocks where he could hide, the shark could not follow. The shark brushed past 'A'aka, its sandpaper skin rubbing a raw spot on his shoulder. 'A'aka scrambled out of the water. His hands were empty for he had lost his rock in his effort to save himself.

His friends laughed for they had not seen the shark. "Hey, 'A'aka, can't catch a rock? How can you catch a fish then?"

'A'aka frowned angrily. "None of you will catch a fish here either," he growled and pointed to the sea. There, just offshore, they could see the dark shadow of the shark as it swam back and forth searching for its lost meal. The Menehune stared at the shark. They had never seen one so big. One Menehune would only make one mouthful for such a shark. And a shark, they knew, would never quit a place until fully convinced its prey was gone. There would be no more swimming or fishing here. They stood on the headland and stared sadly at the shark as it swam back and forth, back and forth beneath them.

'A'aka sat glaring at the shark, grumbling under his breath. Why had the shark tried to eat him? Why not someone else? He felt angry that the shark had chosen him; he was not, he hoped, destined to die as a shark's meal. Flies buzzed about his shoulder where the shark had drawn blood. 'A'aka pulled at a creeping vine to make a switch to brush them away. The vine would not break off and 'A'aka pulled angrily at it. The vine did not break. And then a thought came to 'A'aka. He, 'A'aka, as strong as he was, could not cause the vine to break, so if the vine were ten times bigger perhaps the shark couldn't break it either, and if the vine were woven into a fishing trap, it would be stronger still.

'A'aka looked closely at the vine. It was a huehue vine and its roots were poisonous. Now that he looked, he saw many huehue sprawling under the shrubs growing on the plain stretching inland from the headland. Shouting loudly, he called his friends around him.

"Look!" 'A'aka said, pointing to the huehue, "we shall go hunting for a shark!"

A Menehune named Maliu asked, "How?" He gestured at himself to indicate his small size and at the shark to show its immense size.

'A'aka grumbled, "No, not one on one. A shark is not like a small rock that needs only one man to lift. We are Menehune, we do things together. It is our way."

The Menehune nodded in agreement. Everything they did, from gathering food to building great walls, they did together. One man alone could do little, a hundred men could accomplish anything. They worked as a team under their leader, and as one the Menehune turned to Weli, who was the leader of their group.

Weli said in his deep rumbling voice, "Tell us your plan, 'A'aka. How can we catch that shark?"

"First, we must weave a fish trap of huehue, big enough and strong enough to hold the shark," 'A'aka explained. "Then we must rub the trap with the roots of the huehue to poison the shark. We will need squid to use as bait. Then. . ."

Weli interrupted, "Then we catch the shark in the trap, pull it to shore and spear it to death! Hey, my friends, let's go fishing!"

With much laughter and many happy shouts which made the 'a'o birds bray and caw from their burrows on the headlands, the Menehune broke into groups. One group gathered huehue runners. One group began weaving a huge cylindrical fish trap. Another group pulled up huehue roots, cooked them, mashed them with mortar and pestle, and poured the poisonous juice into a gourd bottle. Yet another group went along the reef catching the squid that seemed to live in every hole. In a short time, all was ready.

"Bring me the canoe!" 'A'aka shouted for he was so excited that he forgot that it was Weli who should give such an order. Quickly the canoe was launched. The trap was covered with the poison, baited with squid, and towed into deep water.

The shark smelled the squid and swam to the fish trap. It bit down on the trap but the fresh huehue did not break. The shark backed away studying this strange object that smelled of food. Seeing a hole at one end, the shark swam into it. Not feeling the cage closing in tighter and tighter the shark made a last lunge and gobbled up the squid. Only then did it realize that something was terribly wrong. When a sharp spear plunged down through the water and pierced deep into its body, the shark lunged forward and swam as hard as it could to escape.

In the canoe, 'A'aka yelled, "We've caught him!"

All the Menehune hung on as the shark dragged them along on its wild ride to free itself. Northward along the shoreline it fled and across the Anahola bay. But the poison and the spear were at work and soon the shark weakened. The shark thought to clear itself of the huehue cage and rushed to the reef so it could scrape the cage along the sharp coral. As it neared the rocks, a wave surged in, lifting the shark onto the reef itself. The huge fish thrashed on the reef, its tail flailing the water into great sprays of foam while its sharp teeth tore at the huehue cage.

The Menehune beached their canoe and hauled the caged shark further onto the reef so it could not escape back into the sea. The little men collapsed wearily on the beach, congratulating themselves and making plans as to what to make with the shark's skin.

They heard a shearwater bray, then another, and from their nesting burrows in the dunes and cliffs around them, the black and white 'a'o whose wingspans were longer than the Menehune were tall, rushed to feast on the rich oily carcass flung up at their doorstep. The 'a'o swarmed over the shark, wings fluttering, squabbling angrily, hooked beaks tearing at the shark's flesh.

'A'aka ran across the reef, flapping his arms. "Hey, get away!" he yelled. "Get away! The shark is mine!"

An 'a'o, seeing fresh food, dove at 'A'aka and its sharp beak tore a gash along one cheek. Weli dragged 'A'aka back onto the beach. "You will have a scar to remind you that you can't fight a thousand birds," he said.

More and more shearwaters were coming, soaring in over the ocean, rising from their burrows in the mountains behind, to join the gigantic feast. The sky was dark with screaming 'a'o fighting for a beakful of shark. Within an hour there were a few bones, a few teeth left of the shark. Only the poisonous huehue trap remained which the Menehune dragged ashore and buried in a sand dune.

Weli ordered a feast prepared and when everyone was seating, Weli announced, "Today, 'A'aka has caught the largest shark we have ever seen. We must name the places where it happened so no one will forget!"

So the places were named. The headland was named ʻĀhihi, Plants-with-long-runners, because this was where ʻAʻaka had seen the huehue vines and gotten his idea. The plain where all the preparations had been made was named ʻAʻaka to commemorate the famous fisherman of sharks. The valley below was named, to the delight of the Menehune who loved to tease each other, Hō-mai-ka-waʻa, Bring-me-the-canoe, for they all remembered that it had been ʻAʻaka who had given this command in his excitement, not Weli, their chief. ʻAʻaka hung his head at this in shame, but Weli clapped him cheerfully on the back and teased him some more. "The place where the shark was eaten by the birds we will name ʻAli-o-manu, The-face-scar-made-by-birds, for only ʻAʻaka would try to fight off a thousand birds!!"

The next evening the Menehune found a tendril of huehue growing out of the ground where the shark trap had been buried. They built a tower of stone beside the tendril and named it Ka-hua-a-liko, The-Place-of-the-Newly-Opened-Leaf.

Laughing and chattering and retelling the adventure of ʻAʻaka and the shark, the Menehune continued their journey of exploration.

As for ʻAʻaka, he never stopped grumbling about the shark skin he had lost and ever afterwards threw stones at the ʻaʻo and kicked dirt into their burrows whenever he could.

NAUPAKA

 he little brown lizard cried out an alarm into the darkness. It was a little sound and did not echo from the black cliffs over Hā'ena's hula school. But Kilioe heard.

She awoke at once, smelling the heavy overpowering scent of laua'e fern. Her sentinel would not have woken her for that. Laua'e belonged to Laka, goddess of the hula, and very soon another group of students would be gathering this fern as part of their graduation ceremonies. Kilioe wondered why the laua'e scent was so unusually strong. Were there specially favored students that she, head of the hula school, knew nothing about?

The sentinel called its warning again.

Kilioe sat up, shoved aside her tapa blankets and went to the door of her house. She listened to the night, the steady roar of the waves surging onto the reef, the faint rustle of hala leaves brushed by the timid pre-dawn breeze. From the direction of Limahuli valley she heard a splashing, someone fording the stream. Then footsteps, receding. No one should be abroad this hour of the morning; there was mischief brewing. Arming herself with her staff of kauila wood Kilioe followed. She could hear the footsteps ahead but she herself made no sound as she strode along. She was tall, taller than most chiefly men and a giant as far as the common people were concerned. Her rigid insistence on the rules and regulations, untempered by any softening to reason or excuse, made her feared. People knew she had tamed the brown lizard to come at her call and, they whispered, she herself was a mo'o, the dreaded giant lizard that could change in the wink of an eye from human to lizard and back again. Kilioe knew this; it was a source of her power. She moved quickly down the path, silent as an owl.

She crossed Limahuli stream, passed the spring of Waialoha, and Maniniholo cave. The first faint streaks of light bloomed in the sky before her. She saw, hand in hand, two figures hurrying across the sand flats of Naue, disappearing within the shadows of the hala trees, reappearing on the white sandy path. Kilioe wondered and followed.

As the mysterious couple rounded the point of Lulu'u-pali, a puff of wind tore the black tapa cloak from one of them. Kilioe realized with a surge of anger that these were students in front of her, students who, by her command these nights before the graduating ceremony, had to cover themselves from the view of all and so were wearing the poloʻu cloak. These were students who had no business being where they were. She following more eagerly, anger flashing from her eyes, her entire body elongated to discover who these two were.

Kilioe was crossing the Wai-niha river as the two went up the path that leads from Ka-lau-heʻe to Lumahaʻi. Now both were visible to her. She shouted their names.

"Nanau! Kapaka!"

The fugitives heard. "Run!" cried Nanau. "We can still escape."

They ran up the hill, down the next hill, swam across the river and onto the green-flecked beach of Lumahaʻi. But no matter how fast they ran, whenever they looked back, Kilioe had gained on them.

Nanau had been planning a way to save his lover and as they came to the cliff in the middle of the beach, he told Kapaka, "Just ahead is the cave of Hoʻohila. Hide there. I will climb to the ridge above and go into the mountains and as soon as I can, I will return. Kilioe will follow me and you will be safe."

He hugged her for a moment and whispered, "May Laka be with you!" Then he turned and clambered up the ridge, making as much noise as he could.

Kapapa, too, had been planning a way to save her lover. She ran for the cave. She stood for a moment looking after Nanau, tears in her eyes. "May Laka be with you!" she whispered. She ducked into the cave of Hoʻohila and waited.

Kilioe swam the Lumahaʻi river and followed the footprints in the sand. She heard rocks falling and saw a figure climbing the ridge above her. With a snarl of rage, she turned to climb after the fugitive.

Kapaka ran from the cave and confronted the enraged moʻo chiefess. "Stop!" she commanded. "Here I am."

Kapaka stood, arms outstretched, blocking the path, hoping to have Kilioe's rage fall on her and give Nanau time to escape.

"Kapu breaker!" hissed Kilioe and swung her staff at the head of the girl. As she fell, Kapaka turned, called "Nanau!" and slumped to the sand. She stretched out her hands in a gesture of farewell as Kilioe struck again. The blood and life of Kapaka sank into the sands of Lumaha'i.

Kilioe clambered up the cliff, intent on punishing the other breaker of her laws. Above her, Nanau had heard the last cry of Kapaka and had turned to rejoin his beloved. If they could not be together in life, then let them be together in death!

Kilioe and Nanau met far up the ridge. She struck with her staff and on Pu'u-o-manu, the hill of the birds, the blood and life of Nanau sank into the soil.

Satisfied with her punishment of the law breakers, Kilioe returned to the temple at Ke'e. Yet that very day news came that disturbed her. The fisherman of Lumaha'i reported that a strange plant, never seen before, was growing on the beach. Birdcatchers reported seeing an unknown plant growing on Pu'u-o-manu. Kilioe went to see these wonders for herself.

Excitedly the fisherman showed her the plant they'd discovered, a shrub with fleshy leaves and small white fruit like congealed tears. And unlike all other plants they knew, it bore only half a flower, neatly divided down the middle, incomplete. Kilioe felt fear brush her like the feathers of an owl brush a rat before it strikes. The plant grew on the spot where Kapaka had died.

The birdcatchers showed her the plant on Pu'u-o-manu. There, where Nanau had died, was a shrub and it too bore only half a flower. Kilioe picked one of these half flowers and went down to the beach to pick one of the flowers there. She placed the two blossoms together and they formed one perfect flower.

Kilioe returned to Ke'e and, kneeling before the altar of Laka, placed the two half flowers before the goddess. The smell of laua'e welled up from a dried fern wreath at the foot of the goddess. The wreath encircled the body of a small brown lizard. Kilioe understood that the goddess had transformed the lovers into these plant forms. Separately they had died, separately now they must live, the naupaka-kahakai, the beach plant, and naupaka-kuahiwi, the mountain plant, their incomplete flowers a symbol of love and of the forgiveness of Laka.

AUTHOR'S NOTE

In the ancient days of Kaua'i, there were storytellers who would sit beside the bonfire of a family and their neighbors or sit beneath the flaming kukui nut lamps in the houses of chiefs. There they would tell tales of the gods, supernatural beings, ghosts, heroes, and real people doing real things. Explanations were given for natural phenomenon, for the coming of the first plants, of the true story of certain rocks. They told stories, anecdotes, myths, history, legends, fables and carried on the traditions handed down from antiquity.

The first duty of a storyteller was to entertain. They were the books, magazines, movies, and television of their day. There were professional genealogists and historians who kept exact records, so the storyteller was free to tell a story in his or her own way.

When the first settlers came, they brought stories with them from their ancient homeland and set them firmly within the places they now lived. Such a story is of Māui discovering fire. Variations of this story are told on every Polynesian island and here the events are transferred to the banks of the Wailua river.

Six of these stories describe the making of natural landmarks. Nā mai'a o Manuahi not only explains the stars of the belt of Orion but personifies the discovery and cultivation of different banana species. Bananas were an important part of the diet and the virtues of proper care of the plants could not be overly emphasized.

Other stories describe how the sands of Nohili began to bark, why the Spouting Horn roars, why a half-flower grows at the beach and its matching half-flower grows in the mountains, why there is a profile of a woman on the flanks of Ha'upu mountain, and of the coming of the first hau tree which was so useful to the ancients.

The rest of the stories in this collection deal with historical persons. Their stories have been augmented by storytellers, who must organize their material so as to tell a good story. Ola lived; place names attest silently to his passing, and the stories here tell of his accomplishments. Palila lived; born and raised on Kaua'i, he left stories and place names behind as he went on to become ruling chief of Hilo, Hawai'i, where his name remains in the genealogical records. Ka-'ili-lau-o-ke-koa lived; her story has become a long romantic novel which has yet to be fully told. Paka'a lived; he became the chief counselor of a high chief on Hawai'i and his name too remains fixed in the genealogies.

I have often been asked where I find the originals of these legends of Kaua'i, retold here and in my first book *Kaua'i Tales*, as well as how I go about shaping them in my retellings.

My sources are far-flung. The Bishop Museum library holds the Lahainaluna Students' Papers of 1885, (Kia kaka o Pā'ā, Ka Mo'olelo o Kahapula), Mary W. Pukui's translation of *A Hawaiian legend of a terrible war between Pele-of-the-eternal fires and Waka-of-the-shadowy waters* which appeared in Ka Loea Kalaaina between May 13 and December 20, 1899 (Ka li'ula o Mana), and Joseph Akina's articles of May 2 and 9, 1913 in the Nupepa Kuokoa, *Ike Hou i ku Lulu-o-Moikeha i ka Laula o Kapaa*, (Palila, Ka ulu mai'a o Palila).

Abraham Fornander's three volume collection printed by the Bishop Museum is invaluable, for tucked into many of the long legends are incidents that make excellent stories (Ka-iki-pa'a-nanea, Palila, Paka'a, Ka paio o 'Opaeka'a). Another storyteller was Westervelt and some of his stories appeared in the magazine Paradise of the Pacific (Polihale). That magazine also printed other legends (Ke one kani o Nohili).

The Kauai Historical Society's papers yielded Judge Lyle Dickey's *The Stories of Wailua* (Ka ulu mai'a a Palila) and *The Portrait of Queen Hina* (Ka pā'ū onaona o Hina) as well as Judge Hofgard's *History of Waimea* (one of many sources for Kiki a Ola).

Unpublished manuscripts contain stories. The history of the Menehune people gathered by William Hyde Rice and now in the possession of John H. R. Plews (Ho mai ka wa'a) and Francis Gay's Place Names collection in the Bishop Museum are valuable.

The Archives of the State of Hawaii has extensive files. Witnesses in a border dispute at the time of the Great Mahele in 1850 gave me a story I have yet to use. There are also papers by Theodore Kelsey and Henry Kekahuna. If all the references to a story in the chants and place names are put together, a legend may be reconstructed (Hina-hau-kaekae).

One legend in this book (Naupaka) was told to me by the late Jacob Maka of Haena.

Out of this raw material, I shape the story following these guidelines: 1) the story has a beginning, middle, and end and stands complete in itself; 2) it should reflect the culture of its time with as few anachronisms as possible; 3) there needs to be descriptions of how the ancients actually went about their daily activities.

Let me take the legend of Kia kaka o Pā'ā as an example. I came across the story on page three of the Lahainaluna students' compositions, Number 1, dated Koloa, September 11, 1885. As given it runs to three paragraphs.

I added the description of the Pā'ā caves from the Journals of Gorham Gilman, written in 1843. Next, I delved into Malo's Hawaiian Antiquities (also a Lahainaluna student's paper) and found a note by Emerson containing a description of octopus fishing and some prayers that went with it.

In rewriting the prayers, I follow Lorrin Andrews' *Remarks on Hawaiian Poetry*, a series of three articles that appeared in The Islander on April 16, April 23, and April 30, 1875. So the story was set in the aftermath of a fourteenth century war and shows how to catch an octopus and illustrates the activities of a priest.

My stories undergo many revisions. My intent is to entertain; perhaps that is why several of them have been turned into plays for elementary school children. I do not emphasize the supernatural as some ancient storytellers did. I try to reflect the beliefs of the times; if people believed that gods walked the earth, then the gods walked the earth because that is what they did, as in the story Polihale.

It is because so many of these Kaua'i stories are unknown, even some that I grew up with, that propelled me into writing. Are these myths, fables, legends, morals, or anecdotes? It depends on the story, but all reflect the thoughts, beliefs, and customs of the ancients, and demonstrate the kinds of stories they thought worth the telling.

As in the olden days, these are stories told to amuse and entertain, not to carry heavy historical significance. Enjoy them.

ABOUT THE AUTHOR

Frederick B. Wichman lives at Hā'ena, Kaua'i, a land rich with legends. He is compiling a list of Kaua'i place names with the facts and stories connected with them. He writes a column for the Garden Island newspaper and is the folklorist for *Kauai Magazine*. He is in the process of writing the story of Kawelo-lei-makua, a ruling chief of Kaua'i in the seventeenth century.

ABOUT THE ILLUSTRATOR

Having grown up in Hawai'i, Christine Fayé has a deep interest in the Hawaiian culture and natural environment. Besides illustrating, she is a stitchery designer and watercolorist.